Ace Trakker

Mark Damon Brooks

Copyright

Prologue

Roswell, New Mexico - 1947

Major Jessie Marcel lights a cigarette as he looks up at the stars. He loves working the night shift. It's serene, especially out here at Roswell. There's nothing else for miles around. Just the way Marcel likes it.

A shooting star streaks across the night sky. Marcel smiles as he drops the cigarette, crushing it under his boot.

"Guess I better make a wish," he says to himself.

World peace? Nah, that's too obvious.

Maybe that promotion to Lieutenant Colonel. That'll do it.

Before Marcel can finish the wish, the sound of footsteps breaks his reverie.

"Making a wish?" Captain Danny Cavitt asks.

Marcel smiles, turning to his friend. "You know I can't pass up a chance to wish upon a star."

Cavitt chuckles. "What is it this time? New duty station? No, you love it here too much. Hmm, let me guess. Promotion?"

Now it's Marcel's turn to laugh. "You know me too well. You owe me a wish, by the way."

"Sorry," Cavitt says, his smile fading.

Marcel waves a dismissive hand. "I'm just joking. I'm sure another star will come along."

"I didn't mean 'sorry' for that. I meant for this." Cavitt hands Marcel a piece of paper. "The call came in just a few minutes ago."

Marcel takes a moment to read the paper, his mood slowly souring.

"You're kidding me," he says to Cavitt.

"Nope. Some local rancher thinks one of our planes crashed in his backyard."

"That's not possible," Marcel says, folding the paper. "We don't have any pilots up tonight."

"I explained that to dispatch," Cavitt says. "They said this rancher is insistent we come check it out."

Marcel thinks for a moment. This isn't the first time a farmer has called in a false claim. Just last month, Old Man Rogers claimed radioactive waste was ruining his crops. Turned out to be the pesticide he was using. This call is likely some kids setting off homemade explosives on some poor rancher's land. Either way, he has to check it out. It's part of the gig.

"Okay," Marcel says. "Who's driving?"

The ride is bumpy yet uneventful. The farm is only a few miles away from the base, one of the closest ones to Roswell. Marcel makes it a point to not really get to know the locals. Other than the cute waitress at the diner in town, he doesn't want to make friends.

Not when he's likely to be stationed elsewhere within a year. Despite his best efforts, he's befriended Captain Cavitt. They both share a love of automobiles and apple pie. It's a simple friendship, but it works.

"We're here," Cavitt says from behind the wheel.

Marcel looks around, seeing a sign that read *Brazzel Ranch.* Next to the sign stands a plump man, waving at the oncoming vehicle. Cavitt slows to a stop and kills the engine.

"You ready for this?" he asks.

Marcel shakes his head with a smile. "Not even a little bit. Let's just get it over with."

They exit the vehicle as the rancher rushes toward them.

"You fellas with the military?" he asks.

"We are," Cavitt answers. "I'm Captain Cavitt. This is Major Marcel. And you are?"

"Mac Brazzel. I own this here ranch. Come on, I'll show you where the plan went down."

"Sure thing," Marcel says. "But first, can I ask you a couple of questions?"

"Or course," Brazzel says, spitting tobacco onto the ground.

"Did you happen to see the plane go down?"

"You're asking if I'm sure it's a plane?"

"Well, yea," Marcel admits.

"No, I ain't sure, but what else could it be? I saw *something* go down. Came from the sky. Guess it could have been a helicopter, but I don't know."

"Have you approached the crash site?" Cavitt asks.

"Hell no," Brazzel answers. "If it was one of your planes, I don't know what it was carrying. Could be radioactive like what happened at Old Man Rodgers' place."

Marcel and Cavitt exchange a look.

"Thank you Mr. Brazzel," Marcel says. "Lead the way, I guess."

It doesn't take long to reach the crash site. Brazzel chose to drive his tractor out to the site, with Cavitt and Marcel following in their jeep. Even with the limited illumination from the headlights, Marcel can see the debris. Lots of it. Something happened here. He's just not sure what.

"I'll stay back, if you don't mind," Brazzel says as Marcel walks past the tractor.

"Sure thing," Cavitt says, his eyes never leaving the debris. Marcel knows Cavitt is thinking along the same lines. Calling out more people. Setting up a cordon. Maybe getting the local sheriff involved if it happens to be a civilian airplane.

"Let's take a closer look," Marcel says.

Cavitt nods as they both walk toward the epicenter of the crash. The debris gets larger and Marcel curses himself for not packing a flashlight. He bends down to inspect a piece of the aircraft while he still has light from the tractor and the jeep. Marcel isn't an aviation expert but this metal is unlike anything he's seen before.

Cavitt shares in his thoughts. "What the hell is this stuff?"

"Not sure," Marcel answers. "Unlike anything I've ever seen."

"There's no fire. No fumes. No smoke."

"Nope," Marcel says. Cavitt is right. Something is off. He touches a piece of debris and... "It's ice cold."

"This is so weird," Cavitt says. "Want me to call this in?"

"Yea, we probably..."

"Did you hear that?" Cavitt says, looking around.

"No. What was..." Then he hears it. A coughing sound, like someone choking.

It's coming from the center of the crash site.

Marcel rushes over with Cavitt in tow. There's just enough light to make out the form of a body. No, three bodies.

"Survivors?" Cavitt asks.

"Maybe, you up to date on your first aid?"

"Yea, you?"

Marcel doesn't answer as he rushes toward the bodies. They're spread out in a small crater. For so much debris, he expected a larger impact site. As he reaches one of the bodies, he recoils in terror.

"What's wrong?" Cavitt asks, rushing to his side. When he lays eyes on the body, he stops in his tracks. "Sweet Jesus."

One of the bodies convulses as it coughs. For a moment, Marcel thinks the lack of light is playing tricks on him. But it's not the light. Not at all. His brain slowly begins to grasp what he's actually seeing.

The bodies, all a very pale shade of grey, have no hair. Two of the bodies lay still, their large black eyes open. Obviously dead. The third coughs again, clutching its chest.

"Oh my God," Marcel says, unable to tear his eyes away. He doesn't even blink, not wanting to miss a second of what's unfolding in front of him.

"Th... These things aren't... human," Cavitt says. He takes a step back, ready to bolt should one of these things moves.

Marcel is far more intrigued than frightened. Sure, he's scared. Who wouldn't be? But this is an incredible discovery. One that will go in the history books. Besides, two of the creatures are dead and the third appears to be critically wounded.

Marcel steps closer, eyeing the last living creature. It coughs again, black blood spilling out of it's mouth.

"What the hell are you?" Marcel says to himself.

The creature's eyes open and slowly focus on Marcel. It coughs again and then... it makes a noise.

"Is that thing trying to talk?" Cavitt says, his voice nearing hysteria.

Marcel crouches down, getting closer to the creature. "C... can you understand me?"

The creature nods once.

"Holy shit!" Cavitt says, running back to the jeep.

"What... are you?" Marcel asks. It's a stupid question, he knows, but it's the only one he can think to ask. His brain is still trying to process that this is even happening.

Regardless, the creature responds.

"Zell... Ita," it says before passing out.

Chapter 1

Present Day

"Are you there yet?" Lonnie asks, making me flinch.

Before I embarked on this hunt, I forgot to turn down the earbud's volume. Now, I'm trying to be stealthy in some dark alley, and Lonnie's voice almost made me jump out of my skin.

"I thought I said radio silence," I whisper through clenched teeth. I add a bit of scorn to my voice, hoping Lonnie picks up on my agitation.

He doesn't.

"I don't know what 'radio silence' means," Lonnie giggles, his voice high-pitched like that of a human child.

I roll my eyes, then take a deep breath to regain my composure. I don't have time to explain to Lonnie the importance of stealth, so I simply say, "Don't say anything until I contact you."

I wait a moment for his reply, telling me he understands. No such reply comes.

"Lonnie?" I say.

"Yea?"

"Did you understand what I said?"

"Yea. I was being quiet until you contacted me again."

I give my eyes another roll, but I appreciate him following orders this time. Now to focus on the task at hand. Catching a Grobelvek. The last thing I need right now are distractions. I take a few more deep breaths, this time pumping myself up for the eventual fight. Grobelveks don't go down easily, and

I need to be ready. I slink further into the shadows, allowing my unique physiology to make me virtually invisible in the darkness. I might be overreacting, but I don't want to take any chances. Grobelveks are dangerous. Dumb. But dangerous. To be perfectly honest, I could stand in the middle of the alley and the Grobelvek probably wouldn't notice. I can't say that for all Grobelveks, but this one appears to be too preoccupied with the metallic sphere it's currently holding.

Part of me feels bad for thinking of this creature as an 'it.' Grobelveks have genders just like humans. Unlike humans, however, female Grobelveks tend to be just as large or larger than the males. Both are equally furry and carry the same amount of sharp teeth and claws. Even if I were standing directly in front of a male and female Grobelvek, I wouldn't be able to tell the difference.

When I run across extraterrestrials I can't identify, I find that giving them a name helps.

I think about what I know about Grobelveks to see if any of my knowledge helps with conjuring a nickname. Let's see, Grobelveks are hairy, broad-shouldered creatures standing approximately six feet tall. They're big. Like big big. Even the smallest Grobelvek puts The Rock to shame.

Does he still go by The Rock? Or is he only Dwayne Johnson now?

I haven't watched any recent movies. Hell, I haven't really watched anything past the 1980s.

Anyway, besides being big and hairy, Grobelvek's facial features resemble Earth's bats. Not exactly, but it's the closest thing I can think of on this planet. Imagine a six foot tall, wingless, bat walking around town wearing a trench coat and fedora.

That's what I'm looking at.

Then it hits me. Rather than going by its physical appearance, which would result in a nickname like BatFace, I go by the disguise it's wearing. The trench coat and fedora. It's like something out of an old black and white movie.

I decide to call it Bogart.

Bogart walked into this alley about five minutes ago. I've been tailing it... him... across three cities now. Unfortunately, there's no hotline humans can call when they spot an extraterrestrial, which means I have to peruse certain social media groups about strange sightings. When I saw #bigfootisreal trending, I knew I had something. From what I could gather from BigD69 on Reddit and SaveTheSnyderverse on Twitter, Bogart was holed up in a state park, likely avoiding humans. Initially, I believed the few people camping near Bogart's hideout disturbed him enough to bring him out of hiding. I quickly learned it was something else. Judging from the camper's cell phone footage, Bogart wasn't really interested in them even as they screamed "Hey Bigfoot!" at his retreating form.

The whole Bigfoot thing is hilarious to me. What humans think of as Bigfoot is actually a species of hairy bipeds called Vangrids who came to Earth thousands of years ago for vacation. When they saw ancient humans walking out of their caves in the nude, the Vangrids followed suit, thinking it was part of the local custom. Now, Vangrids visit Earth every year just to strip down and walk free amongst nature. That's right,

Earth is an intergalactic nudist colony. Oh, Vangrids are also the sworn enemy of the Grobelveks.

If a Grobelvek knew someone mistook them for a Vangrid, they'd kill them on principal alone.

I should clarify I don't just go hunting down every alien walking the Earth. Bogart gave the campers quite a scare, but he didn't attack them. That, in itself, is weird. Grobelveks love violence. What's the human expression? Like a fly to shit? Something like that. That's how much these guys love causing mayhem. The only reason they developed space travel was so they could put the hurt on other species. I wish I was joking. So, for a Grobelvek to encounter humans and not attack, is strange. But just because Bogart didn't attack this time doesn't mean he won't in the future. I have to take him in before he hurts someone.

I wonder, not for the first time, if Bogart's reticence to attack humans has something to do with what he's holding.

From my vantage point, it just looks like a silver ball. Knowing extraterrestrials like I do, it's much more than that. Probably some exotic alien probe or the Grobelvek version of a controlled substance. Whatever it is, doesn't matter. The only thing that matters is apprehending Bogart before his attention shifts from the sphere to unsuspecting innocents. Not that I'm the heroic type. I'm just fixing a mistake I made.

Now here we are. Me, standing in a puddle of what I hope is water, and Bogart standing in an empty alley staring at a silver ball. I wish I could get a closer look, but I don't want to reveal myself just yet. Bogart's furtive glances around the alley tell me he's meeting someone. I'll let them chat for a bit and when they hopefully part ways, I'll swoop in, cuff the Grobelvek, call in the calvary, and get paid.

The sooner I get this over with, the better.

I always hate this part of the job. I made a promise to myself a long time ago that I'd right my wrongs. Rounding up rogue extraterrestrials is the only way I know how to do that. Besides, it's my fault a good portion of aliens were unleashed upon this world in the first place. If I could take it back, I would. Every single time I find one and turn them over to the government, I'm also putting myself in danger. Then there's that small part of me that feels bad for turning in my own kind.

So yea, the sooner I get this over with, the better.

I look at my watch.

It's almost midnight. If whoever, or whatever, is meeting the Grobelvek doesn't show in five minutes, I'm going in. I should have cuffed Bogart as soon as we were alone, but I'll admit, my curiosity got the better of me.

But now I'm getting impatient.

I reach into my pockets, wrapping my fingers around the cuffs. That familiar adrenaline rush surges through my body. I'm not large, physically speaking, and I'm not as strong as a Grobelvek, but I'm fast and agile, which has served me well in the past. Plus, I'm virtually invisible if I stick to the shadows.

I creep closer, Bogart none the wiser. He's still staring at the sphere, caressing it reverently. If it's so important, maybe I can sell it once this is all over.

Footsteps echo in the alley.

I'm moving like a ninja, so it's not me. Plus, the footsteps are heavy, obviously belonging to someone heavy. I pause, pushing myself tighter against the wall. Bogart tenses, then turns to the source of the steps. I follow his gaze.

My tattoo itches. It's a small four-digit number on my wrist given to all prisoners at Area 51. It doesn't really itch. I know it's all in my head. It's my body's way of telling me I'm nervous.

A large dark figure enters the alley, striding confidently toward Bogart. A little too confidently. And is that a... tail? One of my superpowers is identifying assholes at a glance, and this thing is a major asshole. Right off the bat, I can tell it's not human. It's dressed similarly to Bogart, wearing a long trench coat accompanied by a fedora. It tips the hat in greeting and Bogart returns the gesture.

The figure steps into the moonlight for a just a second, but it's enough. I get a glimpse of its face.

I stifle a gasp.

It can't be.

I'm looking at a J'kyrick. A real live J'kyrick. My brain tells me this isn't possible, yet there it is, standing twenty feet away with a devious smile on its reptilian face.

J'kyricks are extinct.

I should know. My family eradicated their entire species.

Chapter 2

I close my eyes and take in a deep breath. I don't need as much oxygen as humans, but the simple act of inhaling calms me. The last thing I want to do around a J'kyrick is freak out.

They can literally smell fear.

I open my eyes, seeing Bogart greet the reptilian creature with a bow. Grobelveks aren't known for their diplomacy, so the bow is surprising. It's likely Bogart knows J'kyricks aren't to be trifled with. While Grobelveks are a violent race, it's the kind of violence equivalent to a human breaking another human's arm.

J'kyricks are way worse.

Like break your arm, then your leg, then your family's arms and legs, then burning down your house.

That's why my family wiped them out. J'kyricks were far too dangerous to roam the cosmos unchecked.

Once Bogart is done with the pleasantries, they get down to business. I don't speak J'kyrick. It's a dead language, after all. I do, however, speak a little Grobelvek due to me taking Grobelvek Language as an elective in college. It's not called 'college' on my planet, but you get the idea. How these two even understand each other is beyond me. Some aliens are just great with languages. Since Grobelveks aren't the brightest stars in the galaxy, I'm guessing Bogart has a universal translator implanted somewhere.

I focus on Bogart's side of the conversation. Maybe I can get some clues about how this J'kyrick survived this long without my knowledge. And what it's doing here on Earth.

BOGART: *My Lord. It is truly an honor. I have the device as you requested.*

J'kyrick: *Unintelligible reptilian noises.*

BOGART: *It was originally found on a human farm. It was later moved to a museum.*

J'kyrick: *Unintelligible reptilian noises.*

BOGART: *I assure you it still works. Would you care for a demonstration?*

J'kyrick: *Unintelligible reptilian noises.*

BOGART: *Very well. Once you activate it, there is no turning back. Are you sure you want to do this, my Lord?*

J'kyrick: *Angry unintelligible reptilian noises.*

BOGART: *My apologies, I meant no offense. About your promise. Will you still honor it?*

The J'kyrick snatches the sphere from Bogart then lets out another strange noise. This one is unmistakable. A laugh. If I had hair, it would stand on end right now. Instead, a shiver runs down my spine. Bogart picks up on it too. He extends his claws, crouches into a fighting stance, and growls. Apparently, whatever agreement they had in place is now null and void.

It's time to end this.

"Stop!" I yell, emerging from the shadows.

They both turn, the J'kyrick's laughter cut short. It glares at me with those yellow reptile eyes. It tears off the trench coat and snarls. I get a better look at it and instantly wish I didn't. Most of what I know about the J'kyrick species comes from my planet's archives. Including appearances. I've only seen old drawings and blurry photographs. Seeing one in real life this up close is a little unsettling. This J'kyrick's face, while having vaguely humanoid features, mostly resembles a crocodile with a much shorter snout. It stands on two legs and now that I'm really looking at it, I can tell it wasn't standing at its full height. Which is terrifying because it's already well over six feet tall. The tail whips behind it, hitting a trashcan and sending it clattering down the alleyway.

"What you doing here?" Bogart snorts in broken English.

"Taking you in," I reply, then point to the J'kyrick. "You're just an added bonus."

The J'kyrick smiles, sharp needle-like fangs on full display.

"A Greymenian?" it grumbles, also in English.

The hits just keep on coming. This thing not only speaks English, but it can see right through my human disguise.

"How do you know that?" I ask.

The J'kyrick merely taps its nose.

Damn. If it can detect a certain species by scent, it can definitely smell my fear. I swallow it down and advance.

"Whatever this little soiree is, I'm putting a stop to it," I say with as much confidence as I can muster. Which isn't a lot.

Bogart growls again, this time directed at me. I forget the cuffs and draw my weapon, which is basically a high-tech taser. Lonnie specially made it for me. It looks like a common human sidearm but it shoots a concentrated beam of electricity. It has various levels of intensity, but I usually keep it set on low. I try to use non-lethal force whenever I can. I don't want to kill my bounties. Sure, they're worth more alive but... and this is going to sound cheesy, but I feel like if I kill them, I'd be killing a part of myself. Plus, they didn't ask for this. They're trapped on this planet, same as me. It's just that some are too dangerous to be allowed to walk free.

Bogart prepares himself to attack, but the J'kyrick punches him in the stomach so hard it sends Bogart sailing into a nearby wall. His hairy body goes slack as he groans and slides to the ground. I fire my weapon, sending blue steaks of energy into the J'kyrick's torso. He flinches but doesn't go down.

Well, that's alarming.

I flick the selector with my thumb, upping the wattage and fire again.

The J'kyrick staggers backwards but remains standing.

Very alarming indeed.

On this setting, the taser should be strong enough to knock out an elephant. I know this because I tested it at one of those human zoos. Not my finest moment.

The J'kyrick charges, swinging its clawed hands. I duck, narrowly missing the attack. I'm not strong, but I'm quick and agile. I convert the duck into a roll and spring up behind the J'kyrick, firing the taser into its back. It roars in anger, then grabs my neck... with its tail.

Where the hell did that come from?

I was too worried about getting clawed to death, I forgot this thing has a tail. The J'kyrick lifts me off the ground as I punch into its abdomen. Again, I don't need as much oxygen as a human, but I still need to breathe. The J'kyrick pulls me in close until its snout is just inches away from my nose. The stench of rotten meat wafts from its mouth.

"You murdered my species," it says.

"Murder is such a strong word," I groan. "Jay. May I call you Jay? I think we've gotten off on the wrong foot. Or claw. Or whatever. I'm Ace."

"You are dead," it snarls.

"Look, anything that happened to your species, you need to take up with the Greymenian Public Relations department."

"Humorous. Even at the moment of your demise, you make jokes."

"You know us Greymenians. We don't know when to quit."

"Soon, it will not matter. This planet will fall. Shortly thereafter, so too will yours."

He holds up the metal sphere. With a closer look, its much more interesting than I initially thought. The sphere still has a metallic sheen to it but it's accompanied by pulsating colors. Every color. It's almost as if the box is all colors at once. It's mesmerizing.

"Ooo, pretty," I croak.

Jay tightens his grip and snarls. Then it does something I've only ever seen in nature documentaries. It unhinges its jaw, opening it's mouth unnaturally wide. Tears pour from my eyes. I'd like to say I'm crying from Jay's stank breath but I'm panicking. The tail bring me closer to the Jay's mouth as thick rivulets of saliva drip to the ground.

Yep, it's official. He's going to eat me.

"Jay, we can talk about this," I say. "All of that happened before my time."

The tail brings me closer still. My mind races. The grip is too strong for me to break free. Doesn't stop me from trying through. I punch the tail until I realize I'm still holding my taser. I aim it at the J'kyrick's open mouth.

"Sorry, Jay."

I pull the trigger. Bright blue light radiates from Jay's mouth. He shrieks in pain, releasing his grip. I drop to the ground and roll away. The taser may not be able to penetrate

Jay's thick hide but it hurts like hell on his soft squishy innards. I stand, ready to fire again. Jay's tail swings wildly, narrowly missing my head. Smoke pours out of his jaws as the air is filled with a sickening burning odor. I fire the taser again, unleashing a barrage of electricity into the back of his skull. He roars, likely more annoyed than hurt, then kicks out, striking me in the chest. Pain flares in my midsection as I'm thrown onto my back.

I try to stand, but the pain is too much. I touch my chest, pulling my hand away to see blood. Jay lumbers over to me, smiling down with a mouth full of daggers. Drool drops to my face. I'd barf if I wasn't in so much pain.

Jay opens his jaws once again. I take satisfaction in the fact that the inside of his mouth is blackened. That satisfaction is short lived as Jay drops down to engulf me. This is it. I'm about to become J'kyrick poop. I've had a good run, I suppose. My only regret is I never got the chance to right my wrongs.

"Freeze! A.I.B.!" a female voice calls out.

The J'kyrick stops and turns just in time to get a face full of bullets. They're a little more effective than my taser as I see bright green blood spray out as Jay roars in pain. He jumps away, quickly climbing a wall. In another second, he's cleared the roof, and then he's gone.

"Follow him!" the voice orders. "Get aerial support here now! I want this entire area cordoned off! One square mile at a minimum! "

A couple of 'yes ma'ams' ring out followed by footsteps retreating down the alleyway. I wince as I sit upright. Bright lights shine into my face. Good thing I have a convincing human disguise or I'd likely already be cuffed.

“You mind?” I ask, shielding my eyes.

The lights are extinguished with a couple of clicks. I have excellent night vision, but even I don’t need the ability to see in the dark to see the three pissed off human faces glaring at me. Besides their similar irate expressions, they also share the same sense of fashion.

"Oh yay," I sigh. “The Men in Black are here."

Chapter 3

"We don't go by that name anymore," Agent Quinn says, her tone flat.

"Oh," I reply with mock surprise. "And what do you call yourselves nowadays?"

Quinn snaps to a couple of agents and points to areas of the alley they missed. She turns back to me. "We go by the Alien Investigation Bureau." Her tone suggests I should have known that.

Maybe I should have. I didn't read the last few alien bounty hunter newsletters.

"Wait," I say, holding up a hand. Pain radiates throughout my body, but this is too good to pass up. "You idiots changed your name from M.I.B. to A.I.B.? And you're still wearing black suits!? What a bunch of doofuses!"

The two agents behind Quinn shift uncomfortable while looking down at their attire. Another one chuckles, which results in an icy glare from Quinn. They all quickly turn away, busying themselves with cuffing Bogart and securing the scene.

I don't blame them.

I once saw Annie Quinn, in a fit of rage, take down a Quaglidite single handedly. Quaglidites are large feathered humanoid creatures with talons that can cut through rhinoceros skin. That particular Quaglidite swung at Quinn, ripping her suit. She already has a hard time finding suits that fit. Not because she's fat. As confusing as human anatomy is, even I can tell that Annie Quinn is... what's the human expression? Jacked. Now that I'm reminiscing, I realize I should not have poked the bear that is Annie Quinn.

Luckily, she's been in anger management classes for the last few months and doesn't take the bait.

"Us doofuses just saved your butt," she says. Another snap and point as a young agent straightens and runs to another part of the alleyway.

"How'd you get here so fast, anyway?" I ask.

Last I checked, the Men in Black are headquartered in Nevada. We're currently in a small city near Boulder, Colorado. That's roughly an 11 hour drive and while I know how they arrived so quickly, Agent Quinn doesn't know that I know.

"It's classified," she replies. "Just know that we have eyes and ears everywhere. We heard about your little Grobelvek problem and figured you could use some help. Didn't expect a J'kyrick though."

"Yea, about that. I had it under control."

"Didn't look like it. J'kyricks are a Threat Level 10. Highest one in the registry. You're lucky to be alive."

"Lady Luck has always had a thing for me." I joke.

Annie, as expected, doesn't laugh.

"Seriously," Quinn says, lowering her voice. "What are you really doing out here? I thought we told you to pack it up after the last one."

Quinn and I go way back. Further back than even she realizes. Quinn started her career of chasing aliens as a sort of corrections officer for Area 51. That's where we first met. She was Officer Quinn and I was Asset# 4. Even then, she had a hard time fitting into uniform. I heard she wrestled in college until she broke an opponent's arm in, you guessed it, a fit of rage. Since the government likes violence, they saw potential in Quinn. She rose quickly within the M.I.B. and I went on to escape from Area 51. Sometimes fate brings us back together. She's only met my newest persona, Ace Trakker, a year ago.

"Can't pack up my life's work," I say, struggling to remember my own human backstory. "These scumbag aliens deserve to pay."

Quinn thinks I'm from Georgia. I never said I was from Georgia. I just never corrected her when I once tried a bad southern accent. Also, I think I there's something in my history about aliens abducting my sister. Or was it my dog? Either way, the abduction is the reason for my current bounty hunting escapades.

"You shouldn't be out here," Quinn sighs. "You could get hurt."

"You tell all the other alien bounty hunters that?"

"They're all far more experienced than you. Some are even former Men in... Alien Investigation Bureau agents. Look, why don't you reconsider my offer to join the Bureau. If you don't like it, at least you'll get some training out of it."

I can't tell if Quinn actually cares or if she just doesn't want to pay me. Alien Bounty Hunters tend to make a lot more money than A.I.B. agents. That's why some of the former agents become bounty hunters. Quinn isn't a bad human so it's possible that she's actually concerned for my well-being. On the other hand, the A.I.B. is notoriously frugal with their money, despite being a government funded agency.

"I think I can manage on my own," I say.

"Oh yea?" Quinn says, taking in my appearance. "You're covered in blood. Is that... black?"

She squints, leaning forward to get a better look. I quickly close my jacket, sending another jolt of pain through my body. My species has black blood, so I can't pin it on the J'kyrick, whose blood is bright green. Grobelveks bleed dark blue, so I hope it's dark enough outside for Quinn to not notice the difference.

"It's not mine," I lie.

The J'kyrick did more damage than I thought. I need to get stitched up before I leave a trail of black blood all over the place. Quinn eyes me suspiciously, then finally straightens with a shrug. While I think highly of Quinn, I can't trust her with my secret. Quinn, like many in her career field, has a healthy distrust for extraterrestrials. Apparently, her sister was abducted when they were kids. Oh right, that was Quinn's backstory. Not mine. That explains the anger issues.

"I suppose you want to get paid," Quinn says.

"That would be nice," I grimace, hiding my pain. "You guys use Venmo or PayPal?"

Quinn snorts out a laugh, pulling out her phone. She taps the screen a few times, puts it to her ear, and goes through a series of security authentications. She holds up a finger, telling me this will take several minutes.

I sigh, which causes more pain in my torso. I grit my teeth, turning away from Quinn to hide my expression and survey the scene. A few more A.I.B. agents have arrived. Some are taking pictures; others collecting blood samples. I hope mine isn't mixed in there. That could end badly for me.

Bogart is cuffed, leaning against a wall, flanked by two heavily armed agents. He glances at me, his large brown eyes filled with sadness. He's going back to the prison we all escaped from. Part of me feels bad. We're not that different. Just two lost souls doomed to roam the cosmos searching for a home. The main distinction being Grobelveks are very violent, while I'm not.

Well, not anymore.

Bogart turns away while a thought occurs to me. The sphere. It's not on the ground and none of the A.I.B. agents are holding it which means the J'kyrick likely made off with it. Maybe I should tell the A.I.B. about the sphere. It could be nothing, though, and I don't want to get them worked up. For all I know, the sphere could have been filled with gummy bears.

They are a delicacy to some species.

Deep in thought, I didn't realize I was walking toward the Grobelvek until Quinn stops me.

"Where you going, Ace?"

"Oh. Um. To question the hairy one. See what he knows about the lizard one."

"Don't bother," Quinn replies putting her phone away. "Grobelveks are notoriously tight-lipped. Plus, we'll find the J'kyrick. It's too much for a newbie like you. No offense."

"None taken."

"Good. Check your bank account."

My fake eyebrows shoot up. I pull out my phone, quickly typing in the various passwords needed to access my bank. The money is there. I'm not sure what the going rate is for a full-sized Grobelvek but this is a nice chunk of change.

I whistle.

"Nice, huh?" Quinn asks.

"Hell yea. How'd you do that so fast? Usually I have to fill out fifteen forms and say a prayer to the IRS gods before I get paid."

Quinn gives me a small smile. "We're trying to be a kinder, gentler A.I.B. Now get out of here. We have work to do."

I don't need her to tell me twice. I'm bleeding like crazy and the last thing I need is for the A.I.B. to discover I'm actually Asset #4. One last glance at Bogart, then I'm half walking, half-limping out of the alley.

"Cabbie," I say into the air. "You got me?"

Of course, a voice replies in my head.

Cabbie is tuned into my brain waves and mine alone. Some might find that creepy but Cabbie doesn't abuse it. He... well, technically, they... only ever listens when I need him. At least, I hope he does.

A black sedan pulls up to the exit of the alley. Over the roof of the vehicle, I see a lone figure across the street. For a moment, I think it's Jay but I immediately dismiss the notion based on it's size. There are a few people out and about, even at this late hour, but this figure stands out. I get the feeling it's watching me. I blink and it's gone.

Strange.

"You going to stand there all night?" Cabbie calls out from behind the wheel.

I climb into the backseat as Cabbie adjusts his fedora. It was a gift I gave to one of the Cabbies a few months ago. I try to give every Cabbie a different gift so I can tell them apart. Aside from their occasional difference in shirts, every Cabbie resembles a portly human male with brown stubble and blue eyes. No matter which one I talk to, they all pick up on the same thread of conversation as if I'd been speaking to that particular Cabbie all along.

The benefit of a hive mind, I guess.

"You don't look so good," Cabbie says.

"Got kicked by a J'kyrick."

Cabbie doesn't flinch. I'm not surprised. He rarely shows emotion. I know he's processing the information, though. His brain... well, brains... are always working.

"Impossible," he finally says.

"Tell that to my mother."

"Fun fact: In the year 1066BG, Queen Zell Onis The Third ordered all J'kyrick eliminated," he replies, his voice monotone. His speech reminds of Data from The Next Generation. I may not watch a lot of movies but I binged countless hours of television while locked up.

"That's not a fun fact," I say.

Cabbie shrugs. "Destination?"

I reach down, opening my jacket. Blood covers most of my shirt. I try not to make a mess in Cabbie's car.

"Take me to Doctor Montes' place."

"At this hour?" Cabbie asks.

"Are you a driver or a question machine?"

"Both."

"Hardy har har."

Cabbie may not emit emotions but he's as sarcastic as they come with a dry wit that can rival the Monty Python crew. Doctor Montes lives in Nevada but with Cabbie driving, we'll make it there within the hour.

Like most things on this planet, this black sedan is more than what it seems.

As the car pulls away, I think about the fight I just had. I've only captured two assets prior to Bogart. They both went down fairly easy. This one, however, was far more complicated. Bogart was into something big. What it is, I don't yet know.

But if my planet's archives are true, a J'kyrick on Earth is a very bad sign.

Chapter 4

We pull up to a modest beige stucco house with a red shingled roof. No light comes from the windows, which isn't surprising. It's around three o'clock in the morning. I feel a little bad disturbing Alissa so early, but she's the only one I can trust to patch me up.

"Your fee is $1,983," Cabbie says.

"I don't have that kind of money," I say.

"Yes you do. Agent Quinn has paid you for the bounty. Fun fact: According to the Alien Investigation Bureau's guidelines, a full-sized Grobelvek earns anywhere from $10,000 - $20,000."

I sigh.

Sometimes I forget Cabbie is in my head. While it's not telepathy per se, it does offer him a unique view into my emotions and desires. Even if he couldn't read my thoughts, his hive mind allows him to be in multiple places at once. There's probably another Cabbie out there working in the A.I.B. accounting department.

"I'll pay you tomorrow, okay?" I say, opening the car door. "I need medical attention."

"Tomorrow will suffice," Cabbie replies. "Please do not be late. Opening a quantum tunnel from Colorado to Nevada—"

"Causes a lot of strain on your quantum batteries which in turn requires a lot money for quantum upkeep. I know."

Cabbie nods.

"You know, putting the word quantum in front of everything doesn't make you sound smart."

"Counterpoint, it sounds cool," Cabbie says.

He's got me there.

"Say, why didn't you just build yourself a ship when I was locked up and get off this rock?" I ask.

Cabbie shrugs. "I like it here."

There are several aliens species that were sent to Earth to prepare it for my arrival. When I was captured by the government, they had no guidance. Some, like Lonnie and Cabbie, hunkered down and went into business for themselves. Others left Earth behind. A few stayed and decided to try and blend in as humans. I'm still undecided on how I plan to spend my the rest of my days. The fact that my family hasn't sent anyone to check up on me is a little disconcerting. Then again, my family doesn't really care about anyone. Including relatives.

I nod to Cabbie then exit the vehicle. In another second Cabbie is gone. I ponder what Cabbie said. He likes it here. On Earth. I never considered this, but this place might be better than his own home planet. I make a mental note to ask Cabbie about it when I see him again. Right now, I need to get these wounds looked at.

I walk to the front door, again feeling bad for the late hour, and ring the doorbell. Being a doctor, Alissa Montes is used to working odd hours. She's not used to house calls though. I stand in the darkness of her porch for a few minutes. Maybe she's already started her shift at the hospital. I turn to leave when I see a light turn on inside the house. A curtain pulls back and I wave at the tired face glaring at me. The curtain closes and a few seconds later, the front door opens.

"Ace?" Alissa says, her face now etched in concern. "What's wrong?"

She pulls her pink robe tight as dark curly hair spills across her face. She tucks a few strands behind her ear and I can see her dark brown eyes full of exhaustion which makes me feel worse for waking her.

I open my jacket. “Had a little altercation.”

Alissa takes in the damage, then sighs as she opens the door wider.

“Come in,” she says. “Go straight into the kitchen. Do not get blood on my carpet.”

I do as instructed, hurrying through the sparsely furnished living room. I once asked Alissa why she doesn‘t decorate like other humans. She shrugged, saying she rarely spends time at home because of work. I don’t have a house. Most of my time is spent between the backseat of Cabbie’s vehicles and seedy motel rooms. If I did have my own residence, I would decorate it just like one of the houses in some of my favorite shows. Family Ties, The Golden Girls, maybe even the bar in Cheers. Not ALF though. That show bugs me. Not an accurate representation of aliens at all.

The TV in the living room is on but the volume is low. I know Alissa sometimes falls asleep on the couch watching recorded soap operas she misses during the day. Right now, it looks like the TV is tuned into a local news channel. I can't hear the news anchors but the ticker at the bottom of the screen reads 'BREAK-IN AT FACEPLACE.'

The image on screen shows a large multi-story building with some of it's windows broken. I've heard of FacePlace, of course. Who hasn't. It's the largest social media company in the word. Not sure why someone would want to break-in though.

Maybe they're mad because their pictures of food aren't getting enough likes.

I cross into the kitchen, jumping up to take a seat on the granite countertop. Alissa arrives a few minutes later, carrying a first aid kit. She looks a little more awake but there's a pained look on her face. Something is worrying her and it isn't me.

"What's wrong?" I ask.

"Uh, you woke me up in the middle of the night."

"No, not that. You look... stressed."

Alissa sighs. "Nope. You don't get to show up here bleeding on my floor in the middle of the night playing alien dad."

I raise my hands in submission. "Sorry. I'm just worried."

"I'm fine, *Dad*." That last word said with a large dose of sarcasm. "Just work stuff. Don't worry about it."

It's hard for me not to worry. I've known Alissa since she was a baby. I can tell it's more than work stuff, but I don't press the issue. She's stubborn, just like her mother. If I pry, she'll just explode and I really don't want to get on her bad side right before she stitches me up.

Alissa sets the bag on the counter next to me, unloading its contents. This isn't the first time I've come to her for medical attention and the bag is packed full of things not typically seen in a normal first aid kit. Mainly, a needle and thread.

"Off my countertop," she says, threading the needle.

"You haven't even inspected the wound, Doc," I say, easing myself to the floor.

"Knowing you, I don't have to. Here. Sit."

She pulls a dining room chair over and I plop down into it. I try to lean back but the hard wood makes it difficult. As

Alissa finishes with the needle, I open my shirt and take in the damage.

Three large gashes run from my stomach to my chest. J'kyrick claws. Alissa whistles, glancing at my injuries.

"What did that to you?" she asks.

"A J'kyrick."

"A what now?"

"Um. Big scary lizard man."

Alissa nods as she goes to work. She cleans the wound with soapy water and wipes away my blood with a dish towel. Unfortunately, alcohol is toxic to Greymenians. Even drinking alcohol. Lame, I know. I wince as the needle bores into my flesh.

"I don't get any pain meds?" I ask.

"I don't have anything strong enough to work on you."

"Just give me the whole bottle."

"Let me finish this first," she says, puncturing my skin again. "So this lizard man. He the basis for those reptilian alien conspiracy theories?"

"Yea, probably. But they can't shapeshift as far as I know."

"Speaking of which, you can drop the disguise. I know how hard it is for you to maintain that."

Alissa is right. I haven't noticed until now, but I've been straining to keep this appearance. I remove my trucker cap, fake eyebrows and wig, then relax my body, turning my skin back to its lovely natural shade of grey. My pupils enlarge, covering the whites of my eyes. My ears shift a little, shrinking and pushing themselves closer to my skull. My nose makes a slight popping sound as it recedes a little into my face.

"Ah, that's better," I say.

"Your disguise is getting better," Alissa says, nodding to my hat and wig.

"Thanks. I'm going for a southern trucker vibe."

"Well, it works."

Not for the first time, I find myself thinking how happy I am that I can be myself around Alissa. First, forcing my skin to resemble that of a human is taxing on my body. Second, it's nice to talk to someone about alien things without them getting freaked out.

Alissa's parents were gatekeepers at Area 51. That's where we met. While kids weren't allowed in the facility, they never kept the secret from their only daughter. They would tell her about me and the other extraterrestrials while telling me stories of Alissa as she grew. I even chatted with her multiple times over a secure video conference connection. Alfredo and Samantha Montes always treated me with respect, almost as if I were human. They didn't believe in how us aliens were treated and when I finally decided to escape, they helped. This house was one of the first places I hid out after the breakout.

"How's your dad?" I ask. "Your real dad. Not me, your alien dad."

Alissa snorts out a laugh, giving me that sideways glance that tells me I shouldn't have asked.

"Haven't heard from him in awhile," she says. "He's been on the run after... well, you know."

"Yea," I reply sullenly.

Alfredo is a good man. Troubled, but he has a good heart. The bulk of his mental decline came from what he was forced to do at Area 51. When he set out to make things right, the government didn't respond favorably, forcing Alfredo into hiding. I don't bother asking about Alissa's mother. That will just start a fight and Alissa is already in some kind of weird human mood.

"So, what's up with the lizard guy?" she asks, changing the subject. "He one of the escapees?"

"Not that I know of. I don't remember him. But Quinn seemed to know about him."

"Well, that can't be good."

"What do you mean?"

"Quinn was part of some black ops things involving aliens. Dad told me they were experimenting with alien tech and biology."

Some of this I know. Quinn and her department reverse engineered alien technology, creating vehicles and weapons not yet seen on Earth. That explains how she and the rest of her team were able to get to Colorado so fast. They have a jet outfitted with extraterrestrial pulse engines.

The alien biology experiments is new to me.

"What were they doing with alien bodies?" I ask.

Alissa shrugs, weaving thread through the last wound. "I don't know. You'd have to find Dad and ask him."

I let out a sigh. I could use my contacts to locate Alfredo, but knowing him like I do, he won't make it easy. When Alfredo Montes disappears, he stays gone.

"He ever mention a metal sphere?" I ask. "About ye big." I hold up my hands, indicating the size. "It has all the colors of the rainbow kind of pulsating through it at the same time."

"Sounds pretty, but no. What is it?"

"I don't know. The J'kyrick ran off with it. It seemed important."

"Ace," Alissa says, her voice now serious. "Let the A.I.B. handle it. You almost got yourself killed."

I wave a hand dismissively. "I'm fine. Tis but a scratch me lady."

"For someone who only watches old movies, you sure do know a lot of pop culture references."

"Blame it on Lonnie. He's always plugged into the World Wide Web. I think he's rubbing off on me."

"Probably a good thing. You need to know about current events. There, you're all done," she says, putting the medical supplies away. "What are you going to do now?"

"I don't know," I lie.

"Yes you do," Alissa says. For a human, she's very good at picking up on alien facial expressions.

"I think I need to figure out what that sphere is. Something about it is nagging at me."

"I'm guessing you won't send Quinn an anonymous hint about it."

"Nah. Whatever it is, the A.I.B. probably shouldn't have it. They've already stolen enough of our toys."

"True. So how are you going to find it if you don't even know what *it* is?"

It's a good question. One I haven't really had time to consider until now. There's really only one place I can think to go for help.

"I have to go see Lonnie," I reply.

Alissa huffs out a laugh. "Great. That's just what you need; more pop culture references."

"He's plugged into everything. Could at least be a start."

"Fair enough. For the record, I think you should just let the A.I.B. handle the breakout. You're putting yourself at risk by facing off with aliens who literally kick your ass. Not to mention also interacting with the government. If they find out who you are, they'll lock you up again."

"I know. But I can't just do nothing. It's my fault there was a breakout to begin with. I have to make it right."

Alissa sighs, rubbing her eyes. "If you say so. Just know that it's not your responsibility. What they did to you, to all of you, was incorrigible. You don't owe them a thing."

"I'm not doing it for them," I say.

Alissa understands my meaning. We've had this discussion before. She eyes me for a moment, the weariness more prominent on her face. Other expressions flash across her features in an instant. Worry. Stress. Whatever Alissa has going on at work or in her personal life, it will probably work itself out better if I'm not around. Just keeping my secret has to be agony for her.

"You can crash in the spare bedroom, if you want," she finally says.

"I don't want to impose more than I already have. Thank you, Alissa. I'll get out of your hair."

I pick up my things and head for the door. I turn the knob, opening it to the cool early morning air. I take a deep breath. The air is heavier here than on my planet. More dense somehow. I still find it quite nice. When I breath, the weight in my lungs is comforting. Like an internal weighted blanket.

"Ace," Alissa calls out.

I turn around. She tosses me a bottle of pain killers. "Don't take the whole bottle at once."

"No promises."

"Oh, and..." She points to her face, making a circular motion with her finger.

“Oh, right.”

I change my skin color back to what humans find acceptable then don the wig, eyebrows, and hat.

“You going to call Cabbie?” Alissa asks.

“Nah. I already owe him like two thousand dollars. I’ll just get an Uber and stay in a hotel.”

“Be careful, Ace. Please.”

I don‘t like to make promises I can’t keep. Greymenians are incredibly honest. Sometimes to a fault. Being here on Earth has taught me how to lie with the ease of a seasoned politician.

“I will,” I say.

Chapter 5

I get to the motel just as the sun breaks over the horizon. After I unwind a bit, I'll likely sleep the rest of that day, which suits me just fine. Going around at night is better for me, anyway. Cover of shadows and all that.

The motel room smells of stale cigarettes and bleach. The plaid patterned carpet is at least 20 years old, complete with 18-year-old stains. There are two beds, both twin sized. I toss my bag on one bed and plop down on the other.

I normally travel light, having everything I need on my body just in case I have to bug out quickly. Before arriving at the hotel, I had the Uber driver take me to all alien's favorite retail store, Walmart. There's two reasons we extraterrestrials love Walmart. One: It's open 24 hours a day. Two: After a certain time of day, just about every shopper looks like a freak which allows us to easily blend in.

With a sigh, I push myself off the bed and open the bag. There's a change of clothes, some basic toiletries. Since I'm devoid of hair, I didn't bother buying shampoo. I do have some soap to shower with and keep my wounds clean. I also bought a few bottles of water, because no matter what planet you're from, you need to hydrate. Also so food, which I guess shouldn't really be classified as food.

I open the bag of Reese's Pieces, dumping the contents into my mouth. Humans usually frown upon this, but whatever Hershey puts in these things is like a porterhouse steak to my kind. Somehow, it provides all the nutrients I need to get through the day. Luckily, I don't have to worry about stuff like rotting teeth and gaining weight. If a Greymenian's tooth gets damaged in any way, it simply falls out to be replaced by a new one a few days later. As for weight, let's just say I've never seen an obese Greymenian.

I tear open another bag, this time eating the candy one by one as I pace the room.

Alissa's words ring through my mind.

You don't owe them a thing.

She's right, of course. I was imprisoned and tortured for years by the American government, as were many other extraterrestrials. I escaped and now have a change to either find a way home or live out my days as Ace Trakker: Alien in Disguise. Unfortunately, it's not that simple. Sure, I escaped but in doing so I paved the way for others to escape as well. Most of which who are dangerous. I could just let the A.I.B. take the reins. They've done it before. Yet there's something inside of me that not only wants to right my wrongs here on Earth, but the wrongs of my family name.

Maybe, in some small way, capturing the aliens I've released will allow me to atone for the things my family has done.

Yea, that sounds stupid. Man, I wish I could get drunk. Stupid toxic human alcohol.

My pacing done, I head to the bathroom for a quick shower. I disrobe, looking myself over in the mirror. Disguise dropped, I take in my skinny grey frame, tenderly touching the scratches across my abdomen. Luckily, Greymenians heal quickly, but I still need to be careful for the next few days. The last time I popped a stitch, Alissa benched me for a week.

Shower over, white bath towel wrapped around by head like I've seen humans do, I head out to the living area and turn on the TV. Maybe something about my scuffle will be on the news. I doubt it, though. The A.I.B. is very good about scrubbing amateur videos as well as blocking media involvement. I spend the next few minutes flipping through the channels, obviously not finding anything relating to my fight with the J'kyrick.

I give up, tossing the remote on the bed, and pull out my phone. A few months ago, Lonnie outfitted my iPhone 8 with the ability to broadcast any television show or music album to anything with a screen or speakers. I immediately and affectionally called it the AcePhone. Lonnie threatened to take it away if I continued calling it that.

Party pooper.

I unlock the AcePhone, then cycle through the menu to my favorite cartoon. The last 30-plus years in Area 51, they only allowed us to watch cartoons from the 1980s. Because of that, I developed a deep love for everything related to G.I. Joe, M.A.S.K., He-Man, Thundercats, and Transformers. My first name, Ace, is even taken from the G.I. Joe fighter pilot. The last name, Trakker comes from the leader in M.A.S.K.

I toyed around with the idea of calling myself McDuck, but I'm neither rich, nor a water loving fowl.

While I fell in love with the characters, able to discern entertainment from torture, some of the others weren't so fortunate. Other Area 51 prisoners saw the exceptional toons as some kind of torture.

Rumor has it, even the 80's cartoons were some kind of government test designed to determine the mental effects on the alien psyche.

Now that I think about it, some of my cell mates did go mad.

Thankfully, it didn't work on me. I'm happy to say my mind is fully intact. The worse those cartoons did to me was turn me into a wiseass.

Bullet dodged.

I settle on Dinosaucers, a cartoon about humanoid alien dinosaurs fighting on Earth, and settle into my bed. I open another bag of Reese's Pieces (really treating myself tonight) and watch a few episodes. The dinosaurs remind me of Jay. Violent. Scaly skin. Lost on a world that isn't their own. Part of me can't blame him for lashing out. He was likely tortured, like the rest of us.

However, J'kyricks are unstable. At least that's what I've always been told. That's what everyone on my planet has been told. Hell, it's in the Greymenian textbooks. They're a violent race. So violent, in fact, that the queen, dear old mom, ordered all J'kyrick's exterminated.

Genocide is never good, but I told myself it was done with the best of intentions. Plus, it happened before I was born, so I had a natural disconnect. I've seen my mother do terrible things, but nothing as horrific as causing an entire species to go extinct.

Again, before my time.

J'kyrick's aren't extinct, though. One has been here on Earth for who knows how long. There's no way to know how many more are out there. There's nothing I can do about it, I suppose.

Control what you can control, Ace.

There's a J'kyrick on Earth. That thought alone sends a chill down my spine.

What are you up to, Jay? What's with the metal ball? Where have you been hiding all this time?

I decide to trust the archives. J'kyrick's are dangerous. The most dangerous beings in the known universe. I'm sure the A.I.B. can handle it, but I can't let this go. I'll do what I can to help. As long as it doesn't get me killed.

Hopefully, Lonnie can help on that front.

These are my final thoughts before I drift off to the sound of animated lizards battling each other for supremacy.

Chapter 6

"Housekeeping!" a female voice cuts through my dreams, followed by a series of knocks.

It takes a few seconds for the fog of sleep to lift.

More knocks mingle with sounds from the TV. More shouts of housekeeping. Before I can respond, the door creaks open. I'm usually more alert than this. I must have been more exhausted than I realized.

The weary part of my brain tells me to just lay here in bed and let the nice lady clean the room.

The logical part of my brain is saying, *get up idiot, you look like an alien.*

I jolt upright in bed, pulling the blanket away as I rush to the door. It opens another inch, causing sunlight to creep through the crack, stinging my eyes. One drawback of having eyeballs that consist mostly of pupil is they let in a lot of light.

A face appears in the doorway just as I change my skin tone to a light brown and retract the blackness within my eyes. I slam into the door, stopping it from opening further.

"I'm good," I say. "No housekeeping."

"Are you sure?" the woman asks. "I have fresh linens and towels and..."

She pauses, staring at my face. I didn't have time to grab my wig, eyebrows, or hat so I hope I just look like a disheveled, tanned, hairless man. But judging from this woman's face, there's something still strange about my appearance.

"I'm sure," I say. "Thank you, though."

I push the door closed to the woman's stunned face, making sure all locks are engaged. I rush to the bathroom mirror to see what shocked the poor woman. Nothing looks off to me, but I've been looking at this same face for over 100 human years.

I need to analyze it like an Earthling would.

I start at the top of my face, working my way down. It doesn't take long before I realized my mistake.

"Ugh. Forgot my nose," I say aloud.

Greymenians can change our skin tone and very minor facial details. For humans, that would be cheek bones, noses, chins. For other species, it could be skull structure, neck length, or ear shapes. This ability to shapeshift... well, I wouldn't call it that. It's more like, shapeshimmy than a full on shift. Anyway, this allows us to blend in with the inhabitants of worlds we invade. Yes, I said invade. No, I don't want to talk about it.

I force my bone structure to change, popping out a rather average looking Earthling nose. I double check my ears, satisfied they look human enough. There. Now I look like a presentable human male. With any luck, the housekeeper will think I was a burn victim or something. I should skedaddle, just in case. The last thing I need is Quinn and her cronies on my tail.

"Cabbie," I say to the air. "Need immediate evac."

Be there in ten, Cabbie replies.

Knowing him like I do, ten means seconds, not minutes. I grab my stuff, once again thankful that I travel light, and rush out of the room. The housekeeper is a few doors down now. She scowls as I hurry down the stairs to Cabbie's waiting vehicle. This one is a red Dodge Challenger.

I climb into the back, sinking down into the seat with a sigh.

"Rough night?" Cabbie asks.

"Rough morning," I reply. "I think I was made by the housekeeper."

"Rookie mistake."

"Gee, thanks. Just get us out of here."

Cabbie obliges, pulling the vehicle out of the parking lot. Every Cabbie looks the same, so I look around for the gift I've given to this particular one. I spot it on the dashboard, a dinosaur bobblehead I won at an arcade.

"Where to?" Cabbie asks, eyeing me through the rearview mirror.

He has this uncanny ability to navigate through traffic while keeping his gaze strictly on whoever's in the backseat. I've been told humans find this unnerving. It doesn't bother me and Cabbie tries to only do it when he has extraterrestrial passengers.

"I need to see Lonnie," I say.

"That will incur a hefty fee. And you still haven't paid for the last trip."

"I know, I know. It's important. You'll get your money. You know I'm good for it."

Cabbie lets out a very human snort, returning his gaze to the street ahead. To show him I'm serious, I pull out my phone and wire him yesterday's fee. I don't hear his phone chime or even see his eyes move away from the road, but he nods and says, "Thank you."

I must have sent it to another Cabbie who let all the Cabbies know I'm paid up. Which brings up a question I've always wanted to ask.

"Is there a main Cabbie? Like the leader of the Cabbies? Oh, a Queen Cabbie, if you will."

Cabbie rolls his eyes and initiates the quantum tunnel. The outside world turns bright white as the vehicle is pulled into some state of quantum entanglement. I wasn't really paying attention the last time Cabbie explained it. Something about tearing a hole in space-time continuum.

Doesn't really matter.

All I know is that a trip cross country that normally takes 43 hours by car, only takes Cabbie about 5 hours.

"We are a hive mind," he finally says. "We are independent, yet we are one."

"Like the Borg?" I ask.

"The who?"

"It's from an old show I watched the other day. Nevermind. So who did I just send the money to?"

"We have a Cabbie who handles our finances."

"You guys are so weird."

"So we've been told."

Cabbie and I make small talk for a few more minutes. He tells me about some crazy passengers he's had, none of them alien. I tell him about why I need to see Lonnie to see if he has any insight.

He doesn't.

After a while, the conversation peters out. We still have about an hour before we reach Lonnie's place. He's holed up in a large storage unit somewhere in Oklahoma. Cabbie seems to be conversing telepathically with his other selves, so I put my headphones on to listen to some music.

Most human music is strange. On my world, we don't have so many different genres. Two or three, max. That could be chalked up to Greymenians not being a very artistic race. Say what you will about humans, they ooze artistry. That being said, there is quite a bit of human music I like. Mostly older music I discovered while locked up.

Alissa tells me I need to get with the times, but today's music sucks.

So I listen to David Bowie's 1972 classic *The Rise and Fall of Ziggy Stardust*. While I mostly listen to stuff from the 80's, I've listened to all of Bowie's albums. I can't get enough. David Bowie transcends time.

As the music fills my heart with content, I ponder my place in the world. This world. Am I doomed to hunt down my own kind for the benefits of man? Or can I live a peaceful life as a human, far removed from collecting bounties on aliens? Honestly, I don't do this for the money. I do it to right a severe wrong. But this has to end sometime and when it does, what will I do then?

I purge the thoughts from my mind. I find it best not to get too introspective in Cabbie's presence. He tends to psychoanalyse and I'm not ready to be honest with myself just yet. One problem at a time. Find Jay, figure out what that sphere is, turn Jay over to the A.I.B., then go out for pancakes.

In that order.

Chapter 7

Lonnie's storage unit is located in Oklahoma City, Oklahoma. I've visited here several times but I don't find the landscape very appealing so I tend to stick near Colorado. In any case, Lonnie loves it here. Something about being in the center of the country helps keep him plugged into everything.

I've dealt with Lonnie's kind before. Almost every planet has. Lonnie's kind are known as Arcnarians and they're absolutely brilliant at obtaining and filtering tons of information. For that reason, they are used as a central information hub for most advanced interstellar colonies. Lonnie was sent here to help me before I was captured and, while he is considered dumb for his species, he can still find anything on Earth as long as he has an internet connection.

"We're here," Cabbie says in a tone that sounds an awful lot like *get out.*

"I get the feeling you don't like ferrying me around."

"Quantum tunneling requires..."

"An enormous amount of power. Yea yea. I know. You know I know. Here."

I tap my phone, sending Cabbie his payment. It's double yesterday's payment. In two days, I've eaten through almost half of the bounty I collected on Bogart. I sigh as I exit the vehicle.

"Thanks, Cabbie," I say.

He nods, driving away without another word. I spend a few seconds taking in my surroundings. It's late morning, far earlier than I expected to be awake, no less out and about. The storage facility is a drab shade of beige with a red metal roof made orange by sunlight and time. A few people are milling around, loading and unloading things from various storage units. Nobody pays me any attention as I walk to the far end of the facility.

Lonnie picked the most remote unit here, for good reason. If he ever needs to sneak around the storage facility, he absolutely cannot be seen. Unlike me, there is no way Lonnie can disguise himself to appear human. I reach his storage unit and tap the keypad. To the untrained eye, the keypad resembles any other standard keypad. When you press a button, however, holographic alien symbols only visible to certain extraterrestrials hover in front of the number.

I punch in the code, then wait for whatever security system Lonnie has in place to analyze me. I once asked him why give me the code, only to have my body subjected to a full body scan whenever I use said code. Lonnie merely shrugged and said, *better safe than sorry.*

The door slides open, hissing softly. I can already feel the heat from inside the unit. It has to be around 75 degrees outside, yet I can feel the warmth from Lonnie's home. His species like it hot.

"Close the door behind you!" Lonnie calls out from the darkness of the unit.

Even with my enhanced night vision, it's hard to see anything

"I thought it closes by itself," I reply just as the door closes by itself.

"It does. It's just an expression."

I can barely make out Lonnie's form, illuminated only by multiple computer monitors. The keystrokes echo off the walls as Lonnie types furiously. Last I checked, he can type 450 words a minute. It helps when you have eight arms.

Or are they legs?

"Can I get some light in here?" I ask.

"Sure thing."

The storage unit lights up, casting a yellow glow on Lonnie's living quarters. It looks worse than the last time I was here, with wires and computer parts strewn about. Boxes stacked high on both sides of the unit and a large hole is in the middle of the floor. To the naked human eye, the hole looks like something done by a jackhammer. I know it was done by Lonnie using nothing more than his arms. Or legs. Whatever.

"You've been busy," I say, pointing to the messy floor.

One of Lonnie's eyes turns back to look at him.

"Oh yea," he says. "Had to upgrade. Built a new supercomputer."

"Does it play Oregon Trail?"

"Funny. Your humor is improving."

"Gee, thanks," I say as I sidle up next to Lonnie. His workstation consists of six computer monitors arranged in a semi circle to accommodate his carapace. Let me clarify that I know a carapace is a shell-like covering similar to what's found on Earth's crustaceans.

Lonnie looks like a giant crab.

Well, a giant crab spliced with a giant spider.

Some might find Lonnie terrifying, but I've dealt with his species before. I find him rather adorable. Lonnie stands about five feet tall when his eight legs are fully extended. About three feet high when he's just walking around... like a crab.

His outer shell is hard and a deep burgundy color. Attached to his shell is a small black box that translates Lonnie's clicks and gurgles into any language he chooses. Today, he's chosen English. We could speak in my native tongue but I told him a while ago, I'd prefer to work on my English.

Rather than having pinchers like a crab, Lonnie has eight spider-like legs, four of which are typing on four different keyboards. To complete his crustacean/arachnid look, Lonnie has eight eyes protruding from the top center of his body. Two of the eyes look at me questioningly.

"Where'd you get all this stuff, anyway?" I ask.

Two of Lonnie's arms twitch in the Arcnarian version of a shrug and says, "burrowed," as if that answers my question.

Arcnarians are excellent burrowers, hence the hole in the middle of the floor. When Lonnie needs something, he burrows underground to retrieve it. I make a mental note to check social media later to make sure there aren't any reports of mysterious holes appearing at classified government facilities.

"How did the Grobelvek hunt go?" Lonnie asks, the voice slightly robotic and high pitched.

"Not good. He was meeting someone. A J'kyrick."

Lonnie stops typing, which is rare for him. I know I've struck a nerve.

"They're extinct," he says.

I lift my shirt, showing him the wounds. "Apparently not."

"Woah. This is heavy."

"I know. I'm sorry you had to find out like this."

Lonnie waves a claw dismissively. "It's okay. It all happened before I was born."

"Still, though. They wiped out your homeworld."

"And your mother wiped them out. So it's all good. Besides, I like it here on Earth better."

"Better Wi-Fi?"

"Funny. Your humor is improving."

"Yea, you mentioned that before. Look, I need a favor. The J'kyrick had something. A metal sphere that shimmered with multiple colors at the same time. The Grobelvek gave it to him."

"Strange. Grobelveks aren't known for their diplomacy."

"I wouldn't say this was diplomacy. More like servitude. It called the J'kyrick 'lord' like it was royalty or something."

"Strange. Grobelveks do not adhere to any forms of government."

"You say 'strange' a lot."

"Because it is strange," Lonnie says, two of his eyes glaring at me. "Consider this. What would cause a Grobelvek, one of the most violent of species and who do not follow any government structure outside of their own, to bow to another?"

"Well, I was hoping you could tell me. That's why I'm here."

"This sphere you mentioned. Did it give off any type of signals? Radio waves? Radiation?"

"How the hell should I know?"

"I reconfigured your phone to detect different signals and radiation."

I can only stare at Lonnie and blink.

"You only use it for music and cartoons, don't you?" Lonnie asks. The incredulous tone is thick even through his translator.

"I didn't come here to be interrogated. Can you help me or not?"

Lonnie sighs, the robotic tone sounding louder than usual. I can't tell if his translator naturally does this or if he amplified it on my account. Either way, he turns all of his eyes back to the monitors, typing on all keyboards at once.

"I'm pulling up your location from last night," Lonnie says.

"How do you..." I stop myself when one of Lonnie's eyes glances at my pocket. "You put a tracker in my phone?"

"Tracker for Trakker," Lonnie giggles. "All phones have them. You don't pay attention to anything I tell you."

"I pay attention to some."

Lonnie giggles again as he pulls up my location from the night before. A 3D representation of the alley appears on one of the monitors. It widens to show the entire block. Blue dots pop up in various locations.

"These dots represent any cameras in the area," Lonnie explains. "I'll try to get a visual on the J'kyrick."

"And see what direction it went," I add.

"Yup."

I watch as Lonnie works his magic. One screen showing camera locations; another showing video feeds. One looks like it's from an ATM. Another from a restaurant's security system located across the street.

"Bingo!" Lonnie says. "I got something from a nearby traffic cam."

"Wouldn't the A.I.B. scrub the videos?" I ask.

"They did. I'm in their system."

I reflexively take a step back. Lonnie is brilliant when it comes to hacking, but the A.I.B. has amazing encryption protecting their networks. I'm pretty sure one of my alien brethren created it but I could never prove it.

"That's dangerous," I say. "What if they track you?"

"They can't. I'm bouncing my IP all over the world. If they did manage to track it, it'll show I'm at some computer kiosk in Seoul."

I shrug, taking his word for it. If Lonnie is anything like the Arcnadian on my planet, he won't listen to reason, yet still provide results. I let him do his thing.

A monitor begins playing the video. It's grainy with a blue tint, but I can make out the details. I see the alley from a different angle and the J'kyrick pop into view on a nearby rooftop. It's holding the silver sphere, the pulsing lights muted through the video. The J'kyrick looks around then jumps to another rooftop, then another. Then it drops out of sight.

"Where are you going, Jay?" I mutter to myself.

"Picked him up the next street over using a security camera from a fast food restaurant."

The video changes to another angle, showing more of the street. A large van is idling in front of the fast food place. Jay runs to it and for a moment, I think he's going to attack whoever's inside. The rear doors open before Jay arrives and a short, hairy figure waves him into the back of the van.

"What is that?" I ask.

Lonnie's arms twitch in that Arcarnian shrug. "I don't know, but it looks like another alien."

"Great. So this thing has two different aliens helping it?"

"Looks that way," Lonnie replies. "Shouldn't you just let the A.I.B. handle this? They already have this footage. They're already on the case."

Lonnie's not wrong. Quinn and her cronies have already scoured the area. They could have missed something, though. Maybe I can find a clue about Jay and his cohort. Listen to me talking about clues like an actual detective. I wonder if Lonnie will make me a fake badge.

"True," I say. "But I need to find out why they're here. Call it a morbid curiosity."

"There's an Earth saying about curiosity absolutely annihilating felines. Probably with lasers."

"I... don't think that's quite right. But I understand your meaning. I'll be careful."

"Is there something more to this, Ace? Something you're not telling me?"

"What are you talking about?"

"You could leave this to the A.I.B. but you don't. You could live out your days pretending to be a human and not chasing aliens, but you don't. Why are you doing all of this?"

"You know why. I have to. After what I've done, I have to make things right."

My tone is harsher than intended. Lonnie knows this is a sore subject for me.

"You're red," Lonnie says, pointing at my face.

Dammit.

In addition to changing our skin tone to fit it, sometimes that same ability will act as an emotional beacon, signaling to anyone nearby how we're feeling.

Red means angry.

I close my eyes, taking a deep breath. I look at my hands; the skin returning to something more human hued.

Lonnie dismisses it with a shrug and continues. "You keep saying you have to make things right, but I think it's more than that. You don't owe the humans anything. Even after what you did."

"Ugh. You're starting to sound like Alissa."

"I'm just saying, make sure you're doing all of this for the right reasons. Whether it be because you are truly atoning for your sins or because you're wanting to be a hero, like in one of your silly cartoons."

I scoff. "First of all, they aren't silly. Second, I'm no hero. This is all about correcting my mistakes."

Lonnie holds up two little claws in a display of submission. He's dropping the subject. For now.

"So what's the plan?" he asks.

"I need to go back there, look for clues, and maybe find Jay. If I can do that, I'll call in an anonymous tip to the A.I.B. That make you feel better?"

Lonnie's carapace bounces up and down. An enthusiastic nod.

"Please be careful," he says.

Now he's really starting to sound like Alissa. Should I be worried? Two of my closest companions are worried, so maybe I should be too. Nah. This is just a simple recon mission. Find Jay. Call in the calvary. That's it.

"I will," I say.

It feels like a lie.

I leave the storage unit, hearing Lonnie go back to his typing. I make a mental call to Cabbie, who informs me he'll be here in a minute. Not an expression. He'll be here in literally sixty seconds.

As I wait, I watch the humans go on with their lives, oblivious to the hidden world around them. Then I notice something. Across the street at a gas station. A figure, dressed in black with a hoodie covering their head. They're looking at me. Could be a coincidence. Maybe just some human checking out the storage facility.

The figure waves at me.

I move from the curb into the street. A car honks as it swerves to miss me, but I keep my eyes on the figure. I don't want to risk spooking whoever it is by giving chase, but I need answers.

Are they following me?

Do they know who I really am?

A car screeches to a halt in front of me.

"Are you trying to get hit?" Cabbie asks.

I look down, noticing the white SUV this particular Cabbie is driving and the seashell necklace I gave him as a gift.

When I look back up, the figure is gone.

Chapter 8

The white pulsing light of the quantum tunnel can be quite soothing. Just moments after getting into the back seat of the SUV, my eyelids grow heavy. Cabbie seems to realize I need the rest and doesn‘t attempt any small talk. He doesn’t even talk about his fee. I remind myself to give him a large tip.

Random thoughts flit through my tired mind. Most of them are about Bogart and Jay. A few are about Alissa and what's troubling her. The most intrusive thought is, who was that person watching me?

To be fair, I can‘t be certain it wasn’t a hallucination. I’m wounded and exhausted and clearly not thinking straight.

Whoever it was knew me. Hallucination of not, that's one thing I can be sure of.

I resolve to figure it out later. One problem at a time. First, I need to figure out why Bogart and Jay were meeting. Then, I need to find out what that sphere is. Normally, I wouldn‘t care so much about an inanimate object, but this thing was passed from one dangerous alien to an even more dangerous alien.

I highly doubt it was something innocent, like an intergalactic Walkman.

I awake a few hours later when the vehicle jolts to a stop. I don't even know when I passed out. Quantum tunneling is just so damn peaceful.

“We’re here,” Cabbie says.

“Yea, I got that,” I say, rubbing my eyes.

I look at my watch. It‘s early afternoon, only a little past lunch. As if on cue, my stomach growls. I haven’t eaten since last night when I had a buffet of Reese's Pieces. I pat my pockets for any extra bags of candy. A brief flash of pain crosses my torso. I almost forgot about my wounds.

"You should be more careful," Cabbie says. "Don't want to pop a stitch."

"Thanks Dr. Cabbie. Got anything to eat?"

"I don't eat."

"You're so weird," I say, opening the door.

Cabbie turns in his seat to face me. I know what he's going to say before he even says it.

"Your fee is..."

"OkaythanksCabbieIloveyoubye!" I rush out of the vehicle, darting across the street.

I glance back, seeing Cabbie shaking his head. I smile and wave. Cabbie doesn't smile often, but his face breaks out into a grin. I don't know if he's amused by my shenanigans or if he's already plotted his revenge.

I'm too hungry to be concerned.

With a shrug, I set out to find some clues and, hopefully, a meal. The area is far busier than it was last night. People walking around, going into restaurants and boutiques. Nobody is aware of what went down last night with the Bogart and Jay. How could they? The A.I.B. are very good at their jobs. It also helps that most alien activity goes down at night. These humans were likely asleep, dreaming about being wealthy or making out with other humans.

Gross.

I walk a block over to where the J'kyrick entered the van, pulling my hat lower as an elderly human passes me with a nod. I nod in return, hoping I don't accidentally have a wild emotion and change colors. I'm usually pretty good at keeping that sort of thing under control. That I turned red earlier at Lonnie's is a little concerning. It has been a long couple of days.

Maybe I just need some rest.

Looking around, I don't see anything out of the ordinary. I didn't really expect to. Even if anyone saw what happened last night, the A.I.B. would have erased their memories... or worse. I find where the van was parked and crouch down, touching the tire marks etched into the concrete.

I tap the tiny bud in my ear. Normally, I'd be worried about contacting Lonnie in public. It looks like I'm talking to myself which could draw attention. Luckily, humans walk around talking through their earbuds all the time. Literally every other person on this street looks like they're talking to themselves.

"Hey Lonnie."

"Lonnie isn't home right now," a voice says, obviously belonging to Lonnie. "Would you like to leave a message?"

"Yea, tell him he's banned from Earth," I say, rolling my eyes.

"Ha. Ha. You don't have the authority."

"Technically, I do."

"Oh. Right. How can I help you, Ace Trakker, sir?"

I smile, appreciating Lonnie's sense of humor. Most Arcnarians are blunt and humorless. Probably because they're under the rule of my mother. She's a big fan of forced servitude, which doesn't really go over well with other developed nations.

"I have some tire tracks here," I tell Lonnie. "Can you, I don't know, track where they came from?"

"Track the tracks?" Lonnie asks with a giggle.

I can't help but smile again. It's good to know he had a relatively good life while I was locked up in Area 51. Who knows, maybe my getting captured was better for everyone.

"Yes, Lonnie," I say. "Can you track the tracks?"

"I can't, but you can."

"Say what now?"

"You have an app on your phone that uses different spectral lasers to find tire treads the human, or Greymenian, eye can't see."

"You're such a nerd."

"Thanks! It's the app with a red laser on it."

I pull out my phone, finding and tapping the app Lonnie mentioned. It opens the phone's camera and for a second; I think I've opened the wrong app. Then I see it. Faint colors dance back and forth along the nearby wall. When I zoom in, I notice what I'm looking at. It's old graffiti that's been painted over.

"Where does he get those wonderful toys?" I mutter to myself.

"Uh, I built it myself. You know that."

"It was a line from a movie. Jack Nichols..."

"What does human currency have to do with this?"

"No, not nickels. Nicholson. Jack Nicholson. The actor."

"Oh yea! I loved him in School of Rock."

"That's Jack Black. You know what, nevermind."

I point the phone toward the ground, using the camera to analyze the threads. More colors fill the screen as blue tire treads extend out into the street, then eventually out of sight. If I'm interpreting this correctly, I could follow the treads until I reach the van. I'm not sure how far away it is, so we'll make that Plan B.

"Hey, Lonnie. Is there a faster way to track the van?"

"Wait for it," Lonnie says, drawing out each word.

The phone chirps, a new notification appearing at the top of the screen. I tap and I'm greeted with a list of... something. I read part of the list, recognizing a few words. They're vehicle models.

"Why am I looking at a list of vehicles?" I ask.

"That's a list of cars the tires could belong to."

"Long list."

"Yea, but I can sift through it and narrow it down."

A thought occurs to me. "Does the A.I.B. have this technology?"

"Yup," Lonnie says. "It's built into a few satellites. Nothing near as compact as what you're holding. Give me a few minutes to go through this list."

"Sure," I say as I pocket the phone.

I think about walking around looking for more clues, but hunger gets the best of me. Hands in pockets with my head held low, I walk to a nearby convenience store. The weather is warm with a cool breeze that feels amazing. We don't have weather like this on my planet. It's mostly what humans call muggy. My planet is very humid, with the air almost as dense as the ocean itself. I didn't even know air could be so crisp and clean as it is in Colorado. Honestly, when I first arrived on this planet, breathing made me a little lightheaded. Now I'm so used to it, I'm not sure if I can ever go back to my world.

Not that I would want to, anyway.

I enter the convenience store, thinking about Lonnie and Alissa's words.

You don't owe the humans anything.

They're right, of course. I could just phone home and have an interstellar Uber pick me up. Mother wouldn't be happy about the progress, or lack thereof, I've made on this planet. At least I'd be home. Far away from humans who imprisoned me for decades.

I'd be home.

I think about that as I grab a few packs of Reese's Peanut Butter Cups from the shelf. The store doesn't have Reese's Pieces, but any variation of peanut butter will do. I just prefer mine covered in chocolate or a candy coated shell.

I'd be home.

I walk to the register and pay for my late lunch. The young man, seemingly perturbed that I've interrupted his comic book, asks if I need anything else. I grab a bottle of water because even aliens have to hydrate, pay for it all, then exit the store.

I'd be home.

Opening the bottle of water, I take in the humans all around me. Some laughing. Others rushing to be somewhere. A few just out for a leisurely stroll with their furry four-legged companions. Dogs, I've been told, make noble companions. On my world, we have something similar. Grangus are what you get if you cross a cat with an iguana, then add a touch of raccoon. And they have the intelligence of a chimpanzee. While cute, they can cause a lot of trouble if not properly trained.

I'd be home.

I don't want be home.

The realization hits me like a ton of bricks. Is this why I'm so hellbent on catching the Area 51 escapees? Even if that's the case, it doesn't matter. I'm just delaying the inevitable. Greymenians live a very long time and our memories live even longer. Someone will come for me.

Eventually.

Maybe they already have.

The mysterious figure I've seen twice now could be a Greymenian scout reporting back to my mother. I finish the water, toss the bottle in a nearby trash can, and rip open pack of the peanut butter cups. I toss one into my mouth as I contemplate my next move.

Give up this J'kyrick chase and go into hiding. Yea, that seems like the best bet. The A.I.B. can handle Jay. They don't need me. So that's it, then. I'll have Lonnie forge yet another fake identity then I'll move to Canada or something and get a job at a candy store. Unlimited supply of food. Can't beat that.

"I've got something," Lonnie says.

"I was just about to call you," I say. "I need a new..."

"I think I found the truck," he blurts out.

My dreams of being a Canadian candy connoisseur will have to wait.

"Where is it?" I ask.

"I cross-referenced the tires with any vehicle fitting the description of the van. Naturally, that yielded a bunch of results. Lot of companies with white vans that use that brand of tire. Anyway, I narrowed it down to just the companies near you. That gave me seven companies. Five of them use different color vans now. Another went out of business. That leaves one last company, a junkyard close to your location. Sending it to your phone now."

My phone chirps.

I pull the phone out and tap on Lonnie's notification. A map appears with a red arrow showing the junkyard and a green line showing the route. It's maybe a fifteen minute drive away. No need to get Cabbie involved.

"Thanks," I tell Lonnie. "I'll go check it out. Can you get schematics of the building?"

"It's old. Like old old. Also, it looks like it's been changed numerous times over the years. I can get you something, but it won't be up to date. Plus, all the junk there makes the entire area a maze."

"Just do what you can and send it as soon as possible."

"Will do. Lonnie out."

The line goes dead and I open up the Uber app to get a ride. This will be much cheaper than calling Cabbie. Even without quantum tunneling, he charges me a crazy amount. I wonder if he charges his human riders the same.

I'd be home.

Even if I wanted to go home, I can't. Not with unfinished work to do. I could kick myself for being so self righteous. If Mother saw me now, she'd probably have me executed. I wasn't sent to this planet to be a protector. Quite the opposite, actually.

Maybe my imprisonment changed me. Maybe I was never really down with the family business to begin with. All I know is that it actually feels good to do something I want to do.

And right now, I want to find Jay and figure out what the hell he's up to.

Chapter 9

Lonnie was right. The junkyard is a literal maze. A fence surrounds the entire area which is roughly ten acres. I'm guessing the fence is there more for keeping stuff in, rather than out. Old rusted cars and miscellaneous junk are piled high and randomly strewn about. Someone thoughtfully stacked the junk in such a way that various paths snake around the compound. Luckily, scaling the fence was easy.

Now I'm slowly making my way to the main building at the center of the junkyard. If you would have told me a day ago I'd be surrounded by old human junk, I would have laughed in your face. I keep my eyes peeled for danger, but I can't help but admire the junk. Old washing machines. refrigerators, televisions. It becomes a game as I walk. Identify that piece of junk. So far, I've successfully identified twenty different pieces of junk. So I guess I win the game. It's a lot easier when you're the only player.

I turn a corner and pause. A few meters ahead, I can barely make out the wooden shack. I duck behind a pallet of old toaster ovens and scan the area. At a glance, I see nothing amiss. Just a few people milling about, tearing various parts off of various things. One whoops loudly as if he's just discovered gold.

It takes me a minute to realize they aren't people. They all have the same build as the figure we saw on the video in the back of the van.

Great, more aliens to deal with.

At least Lonnie‘s description of the building was pretty spot on. It looks like it used to be an old wooden shack that was later lengthened with metal paneling. There are a couple of windows but they’re so dirty I can’t see inside.

I pull out my phone and shoot a text to Lonnie.

ACE: Does this phone have an x-ray app?

LONNIE: Like Superman?

ACE: What‘s a Superman?

LONNIE: Only the coolest alien ever!

ACE: Never heard of it.

LONNIE: Him. Not it. Oh, my Frolgar. Read a comic every now and then.

ACE: What‘s a comic?

LONNIE: I don‘t have time for this. Yes, there is an x-ray app. It’s the app titled X-RAY.

I scroll through the apps and sure enough, there it is.

Well, I‘ll be damned.

I click it, testing it by hovering the camera above my hand. White bones shine through the dark grey outline of my skin.

“Neat,” I whisper to myself.

I raise the phone, aiming the camera at the shed. The area now bathed in muted colors. The junk even more undisguisable from each other. The three employees outside turn into walking skeletons, their bones thick and distorted further proving they're extraterrestrial.

“Double neat.”

I focus on the building, not seeing any changes. Maybe there‘s a different setting to penetrate through the walls. I check the app, not finding anything that will make any changes. I shake the phone, knowing that won't work, but it does aid with my frustration.

I text Lonnie again.

ACE: Hey punk. X-ray app doesn't work.

LONNIE: It works. You're just a moron.

ACE: First, ouch. Second, I tried it and can't see inside the building.

LONNIE: LOL! It doesn't work on buildings, you big grey dummy!

ACE: You said it was an X-ray app!

LONNIE: Yea! For skin! Not brick or metal or wood.

ACE: I hate you.

LONNIE: I hate you, too. Bye!

Well, that plan is out. I pocket the phone with a sigh and ready myself for whatever comes next. Without knowing how many hostiles are in the building, I can't be certain that sneaking in would be safe. I can try to camouflage my skin but immediately dismiss the notion because of the varying colors and patterns making up the building. I can only focus on one color at a time. If I can find a shadowy spot, maybe, just maybe, it will work.

Either way, I have to figure out what's going on inside.

One of the employees, seemingly happy with some fresh crap they just salvaged, walks inside the building. That leaves two outside, still happy to rummage through garbage. They're distracted so I can take them by surprise. Yea, that's the plan. Take these two down, then head inside all quiet like.

I can take two measly aliens.

Right?

Of course, I can.

I think I'm just feeling a little apprehensive since I got my zorax, or what's known as an ass to humans, handed to me yesterday by a big scaly lizard monster.

"Take a deep breath, Ace," I mutter to myself. "You got this."

I inhale deeply, then stretch to loosen my joints. I don't really need to do this since Greymenian bodies don't require warming up. Seriously, I could run a five-mile sprint from a full stop and never get a cramp. But I've seen humans do it and it seems to put them at ease before they do something stupid.

When on Earth, do as the Earthlings do.

I draw my taser, setting it to a level that I hope will comfortably subdue these aliens without killing them. I crouch, slowly weaving between junk. One employee is turned away from me, but at this range I can make out more details. They're short and stocky, with arms as big as my waist. Tufts of back hair protrude from their shirt, making me gag. Us Greymenians pride ourselves on our lack of body hair. The other employee looks the same. Short, overweight, with enough body hair to make Bigfoot jealous.

The two employees look exactly the same.

Humans call this phenomenon 'twins.' My extraterrestrial brain knows better. Seeing two beings who look exactly the same is a pretty normal occurrence for me. Hell, I ride around with a hive mind Uber driver who clones himself. At least I think they're clones. I haven't figured that out yet.

I aim the taser at the one closest to me, praying it will be strong enough. Just as I'm about to pull the trigger, one turns to me and growls.

Like, literally growls.

"Shit," I say, pulling the trigger.

The shot goes wide, striking a pile of car parts. The first one lunges while the other turns, confusion on its pug-like face. I know what these things are now. Grunkles. Universal trash haulers. Makes sense they'd be in a junkyard on Earth. These guys love trash.

I dive to my right, letting the lunging Grunkle pass by. While he's getting his bearing, I shoot the second one; the blast knocking him back a couple of feet.

He's still standing.

"What the..."

Then I remember I set the taser too low, hoping not to kill anyone. Of course a Grunkle will withstand it. Grunkles are a scavenger race, building ships and cities out of other species' junk. They're brilliant mechanical engineers, but not very smart at anything else. They resemble just about any short, fat, hairy human male you've ever seen, except they can extend their claws at will and their eyes are just a shade too red to be normal. If anyone glances at one, they would just think they were out all night drinking.

"Fellas. We can talk about this," I say, attempting to discreetly crank up the settings on my taser.

Grunkle One charges again. I jump out of the way just as Grunkle Two picks up a jagged metal object to swing at my head. I roll to my feet, twisting my body like a contortionist to dodge the blow. The metal grazes my head, but I avoid the worst of it. Grunkle Two stumbles on the downswing and I see my opening. I kick him in the back, which causes me to flop on my zorax. He stumbles but stays on his feet.

Grunkle One pushes his buddy out of the way, bloodlust in his eyes. He rushes me, lashing out at me with newly extended claws.

I didn't even know Grunkles were on this planet. Now I'm dodging one trying to claw me to death. That's the second alien in as many days that I knew nothing about.

Getting kind of tired being the last one in the know.

I take a few steps back, dodging Grunkle One's claws. My back hits something, stopping me in my place. Grunkle One swings again. I raise my taser to fire but only succeed in blocking the swing. Sparks fly as his claws hit the metal. I lean back on whatever stopped me, using it as leverage as I kick out with both feet, nailing Grunkle One in the chest. He falls on his backside with an *oompf* as Grunkle Two rejoins the fight.

I quickly turn up the taser and fire. Grunkle Two convulses, then drops to the ground. Grunkle One roars, jumping to his feet. I dodge another volley of swings, trying to put enough distance between us so I can safely electrocute this fool.

Then Grunkle One changes tactics, going low and rushing me with a surprising display of speed. I'm slammed into more junk causing the taser to drop from my hand. Bits of dirt and debris rain down on us as I struggle to free myself. Grunkle One squeezes me in a bear hug, forcing the air from my lungs. I elbow him in the back, but his skin is too thick to make a difference. I feel around the junk for anything useful as he continues to squeeze. Darkness encroaches on my vision. My hand brushes something hard and metallic. I pull on it, feeling its weight. It'll have to do. I swing it at Grunkle One's head. He staggers a bit, loosening his grip. I hit him again, harder this time. He release me, putting a hand to his head. I drop to my knees, scooping up the taser and firing it into his chest.

Grunkle One slumps to the ground, finally down for the count.

The taser sparks, burning my hand. I drop it with a yelp and look around to be sure we weren‘t heard. Everything appears to be clear. I suck in a lung full of air, feeling pain in my abdomen as it expands. I still haven’t fully healed from Jay’s kick. Another ten seconds in Grunkle One’s grasp and I would have been unconscious. Then who knows what would have happened. I brush myself off, shakily rising to my feet. Blood seeps through my shirt. I must have torn some stitches.

I can‘t worry about it now.

I‘ve had enough close encounters with death for the day. Now that I know these aren’t human, I should be able to easily take down the third Grunkle.

I pick up the taser, inspecting the damage. The Grunkle claws tore away bits of metal, revealing the wiring beneath. Unfortunately, I don‘t have the repair kit and even if I did, I likely wouldn’t have enough time to fix it with Grunkle Three inside.

I walk to the entrance, opening the door a crack. I hear noises deep within the building. Voices. Aliens voices. Some low shrieks and grunts. It almost sounds like an argument. Without a weapon, I‘m not sure I can take on another Grunkle, let alone Jay. I have to play this smart.

Stealth it is.

Chapter 10

I slip inside the door, immediately adjusting my vision to take in more light. The place isn't dark, but there are enough shadows to give me pause. Better to be safe than sorry. As I creep further into the building, it's hard to tell what's an actual wall or just a pile of junk. If it weren't for the roof, I'd think I was still outside amongst the skyscrapers of damaged cars and rusted washing machines.

The smell hits my nostrils first. Motor oil, body odor, and rotting food permeate the air. I contort the bones in my face to flatten my human nose. It doesn't help against the smell, but it makes me feel better. I struggle not to gag as I move further into the building.

The voices grow louder as I continue to inch closer. I consider darkening my skin to blend into the shadows better, but my blue jeans and Jurassic Park t-shirt would likely standout. If anyone sees me, a hasty exit is probably the best bet.

Cabbie, you got me? I think.

Already in route, he replies.

You're my favorite. Don't tell Lonnie.

It will be our little secret.

Knowing Cabbie will be outside soon eases my nerves a bit. If things go south, I just hope I can make it out of here in time. This place is just as much of a maze as outside. The hallway, at least I think I'm in a hallway, leads to a larger open area. From here, I can see cars and other vehicles I don't recognize hanging from chains. There's also a few parts from alien ships

I recognize. It's a workshop of some kind. Much larger than it looks from outside.

I strain to focus on the voices. One is obviously a Grunkle, their guttural tone echoing down the hall. Another voice, more cultured yet far more terrifying.

I stiffen.

"You promised it would be ready," Jay says, not even trying to conceal his anger.

Or maybe that's how he always sounds. Something tells me J'kyricks always sound angry.

"My Lord," Grunkle Three says. "Give us more time. We are still acquiring the parts."

"I don't want your excuses!" Jay roars.

A crashing sound tells me he's smashed something. Maybe the Grunkle. The next reply tells me the Grunkle is still standing.

"No excuses, My Lord. We are but a small crew. And Earth's technology is not yet advanced enough to..."

Another crash. Grunkle Three lets out a yelp. I can't see what's going on, but I'm sure Jay is giving him the beat down. Again, I'm stuck by the words used to address Jay. The Grunkle called him 'Lord,' the same as Bogart. Two different alien races addressing this thing with the utmost respect. Sure, he's threatening to kill them, but there's something else to it. Something familiar I can't quite put my finger on.

I'll have to focus on it later.

"My Lord," Grunkle Three croaks.

Something about the tone tells me Jay is pulling a Darth Vader. Except instead of using the Force, Jay is likely choking the Grunkle with his tail.

"We are working as hard as we can," Grunkle Three continues. "Please. I understand your frustrations. We simply don't have the resources."

I unconsciously rub my neck, remembering Jay choking me just a day ago. Grunkles can be real jerks sometimes, but I wouldn't wish that pain on them. My thoughts drift for a second as I wonder if Jay's tail will grow back if dismembered. Obviously, if I had a sword, I could test that theory. Note to self: have Lonnie forge me my very own Sword of Greyskull.

"Then get the resources," Jay snaps, breaking me from my reverie. "I will grant you one more day."

"Yes My Lord," Grunkle Three says, gasping for air. "It will be done."

One more day for what, I wonder. I've always thought J'kyricks were dumb and feral, but Jay is clearly intelligent. Given his propensity for violence, however, I still have to treat him as a threat. I already know I can't take Jay alone, but maybe there's something here that can help. If I know Grunkles, then they'll have a stash of modified alien weaponry somewhere around here. The problem is, this place is such a mess, it'll take me ages to find it.

I could just leave and come back later when Jay is gone. Have Lonnie repair my taser, then return to question the Grunkles and hopefully put an end to whatever Jay is planning.

I slowly back away from the workshop.

"Who else is here?" Jay asks, suddenly.

I tense. I didn't make a sound. Did I? I'm basically an alien ninja so if Jay knows I'm here then something else is at fault. Probably the shoes. Stupid human shoes with their rubber soles.

"Just my brothers and I," Grunkle Three replies.

"No. There is another."

A series of creaks tells me either Grunkle Three or Jay are moving across the wooden floor. The increasing loudness of the creaks tells me someone is moving this way. I hold my breath, darkening my skin to blend in then rush to the exit as silently and quietly as I can.

I hope Cabbie is waiting.

I'm here, Cabbie says, reading my mind. *But there's a disturbance.*

What do you mean?

There's...

Before he can finish, the J'kyrick rushes around the corner and pauses, sniffing the air. He's just inches away, but he's not tearing me to shreds. I risk looking into his eyes to see they aren't focused on me. his eyes don't drift to me. Jay rushes past me, tearing the front door from its hinges. Sunlight floods the hallway, burning my eyes.

The sound of gunshots rings through the missing door.

Cabbie, what the hell is going on out there?

As I stated earlier. A disturbance.

I roll my eyes. Cabbie can be very literal sometimes. Normally I don't mind, but it sounds like a war is popping off outside and NOW IS NOT THE TIME.

Might have to rethink making Cabbie my favorite.

What is the disturbance? I try again gently, struggling to control my internal tone.

Agent Quinn has engaged the J'kyrick. Rather, the J'kyrick has engaged the A.I.B.

Great. That's the last thing I need. I arrange my face and skin back to that of a normal human and peek out of the entrance. Just like Cabbie said, the A.I.B. is here complete with a ground team and helicopter.

Something tells me it won't be enough.

"Game over, man," I whisper to myself. "Game over."

Chapter 11

A thought a occurs to me. That little nagging sensation in the back of my brain that tells me I really should hide or, at the very least, escape out the back. The dumber part of my brain, the part that gets me into situations like these, wants to see this through. I'm sure the A.I.B. has what it takes to handle Jay. I know I sure as hell don't. Besides, this time, Jay doesn't really have anywhere to go. He's trapped by the high walls of garbage and there's a platoon of A.I.B. agents outside.

Ah, what the hell.

I decide to stick around. Not out of some sense of nobility, but because I'm just as trapped as Jay. Even if I escape, the helicopter will pick up on my heat signature, alerting the other agents. Then I'd be in big trouble. Better just stay put and face the music.

As if proving my point, Grunkle Three yelps at a nearby explosion and rushes out the rear exit. I almost forgot he was here, but he's not worried about me. I doubt he even realizes I'm in the building. Grunkle Three yelps again as A.I.B. agents descend on him, cuffing him and carrying him out of view. I know they're only seconds away from sweeping the building. I make sure I have my human face on and hold my hands in the air.

I hate to tear my eyes away from the battle outside, but I also don't want to get shot in the back. Agents pour in from the rear exit, weapons raised. They're decked out in their usual black body armor that looks way more futuristic than anything any other government agency. Housing aliens for the last several decades has had its benefits. One of which being free labor from species who have mastered interstellar space travel.

That armor can likely survive a ballistic missile.

"Hands up!" an agent yells, weapon aimed at my torso. His face is partially hidden behind protective glass. It's slightly tinted, but I can see the corner of his mouth twitch slightly. He's struggling to not show how much he's enjoying this.

"My hands are already up," I reply.

"Hands up!" another agent cries.

I sigh, raising my hands even higher. I count three agents covering me and hear several more rummaging through the building. An agent approaches me, grabbing my wrists and twisting my arms behind my back. I can tell he's muscular, even through the armor. He cuffs me while the other agent, an almost equally muscular female, covers him. Then he tosses me to the ground, pushing a knee into my back.

"Don't move," the female agent warns.

I instantly recognize the voice.

"Hey Annie," I groan.

She kneels down to get a better look at my face. Even through the glass faceplate, I see her eyes roll.

"What the hell are you doing here, Ace?" Quinn asks.

"Would you believe buying some parts for a '67 GTO?"

"No." She motions to the other agents. "Get him up."

I'm pulled to my feet as Annie looks me over. Blood pours from my torso wounds. Hopefully, my shirt is dark enough to hide it. Annie doesn't react. If she notices the blood, she doesn't mention it.

"You look like shit," she says.

"And you look enchanting, as always."

She snorts a laugh, then walks to the entrance. Knowing Annie, she‘s itching to join the fight. She was intimidating before, but now, in the black body armor, she scares the hell out of me. Annie is large. And I don’t mean in that she’s eaten too much fast food kind of large. She’s roughly 6 foot 2, with broad shoulders that are likely brought about by genetics but enhanced by hours in the gym. The last time I saw her, she was wearing the A.I.B. standard black suit, and it was stretching at the seams.

I try to stay on her good side.

“Annie, where you going?” I ask, playing dumb.

“To help my team,” she says. “Then we’ll deal with you.”

“Can you guys at least carry me to a window or something so I can see the action?”

Annie considers it for a second, then nods at the two agents detaining me. They half drag, half carry me to the open door just as Annie walks outside, disappearing into the blinding sunlight. They stay by my side, both gripping each of my arms tight. Once my eyes adjust, I see the battle raging outside. Jay jumping from one trash pile to another, dodging bullets and energy weapons. He uses the junk as weapons, tossing a muffler at a nearby agent, who dodges it with inhuman speed. I'm guessing the armor does more than protect their bodies.

The helicopter swings into view overhead as the agents engaging Jay back away. Jay roars at the chopper, readying another piece of junk to throw. The helicopter doesn't wait for Jay to attack and unleashes a volley of rockets into his body. The explosions tear apart the junk piles, tossing debris into the air. I flinch as metal rains down in front of me. The two agents at my sides stand perfectly still, letting the debris ping off of their armor. I open my eyes again, hardly believing what I just saw.

"You guys have rocket launchers?" I ask, breathless.

"Standard issue," one agent replies simply, like I just asked what he's eating.

When the smoke clears, Jay's body is nowhere to be found. A couple of agents whoop in celebration. I wince, knowing the celebration will be short-lived. J'kyricks are extremely resilient. Judging from the archives, the only way to fully ensure they were dead was to destroy their entire planet.

A reptilian arm rises from the rubble.

I hate to say I told you so...

Annie yells something I can't hear and the remaining agents open fire. Their bullets don't seem to do much, but the rounds from the helicopter's mini guns tear a few chunks of flesh from Jay's torso. Not nearly enough, though.

Damn, these things are tough.

Jay roars again, lifting the rusted husk of a vehicle and tossing it into the air. The helicopter swerves to dodge it, but it's too late. Glass shatters as the car hits the cockpit, causing the helicopter to spiral out of control. Seconds later, it crashes behind a wall of junk. The impact shakes the ground as a fireball rises into the air. The split second of shock from the A.I.B. agents is all Jay needs. He picks up another piece of junk, tossing it at the nearest agents. They don't notice it in time and are knocked to the ground.

Annie and the other agents don't let up, all firing directly at Jay. He growls at them, then his eyes flick to me standing in the doorway. Recognition crosses his reptilian features and a chill goes down my spine. His eyes narrow, his hatred palpable.

He turns away from Annie and her team, climbing a nearby wall of junk and disappearing deeper into the junkyard. Without air support, they have no choice but to let Jay go. For now.

The remaining agents rush to aid their comrades. Most of the agents appear to be fine. Unfortunately, those in the helicopter are likely dead, but that doesn't stop a few agents from heading in that direction.

The agent to my right says something. I'm guessing he's talking to someone on the comms in his helmet. I can barely make out, "Yes ma'am, we still have him."

They're talking about me.

Uh-oh.

Annie strides over, her gait even more intimidating than usual. I can tell by her body language she's pissed. I can't blame her. Her team just got their asses kicked by a J'kyrick. One agent pushes me out of the entrance until I'm face to face with Annie Quinn. She removes her helmet, her red hair pulled tight into a bun. Probably not a good idea to have hair in your eyes when you're fighting deadly extraterrestrials. Another reason I'm glad I don't have that problem.

"Time to tell me the truth, Ace," Annie says, her voice oozing with contempt. "What the hell do you know about that thing?"

"The J'kyrick? Nothing that I haven't already told you before. I was tracking a Grobelvek when the J'kyrick showed up. I tried to take it down too, but it kicked my butt. Then you all showed up and saved me."

"And what are you doing here?"

"I thought I could catch it and get paid," I lie. "I'm not sure what the bounty is on a beast like that, but it's gotta be huge."

Annie thinks it over. Wondering if I'm full of it or not. I am. She just doesn't know how much.

"How'd you get here?" she finally asks.

"I have a friend who does IT stuff. He hacked into some street cams and got the license plate. I tracked it to this junkyard."

Annie nods, then waves a hand at the two agents detaining me. "Take him to HQ for questioning."

My chest tightens. The Alien Investigation Bureau is the last place I want to be right now.

"Um. Can't we talk about this? I pay my taxes." I don't. "We don't have to go through all this. Look, I'll keep my nose out of it from now on."

If they take me in for questioning, they might take my fingerprints or my blood. As soon as my inked up finger hits that piece of paper, they'll know. Greymenians have fingerprints, like humans, it's just that ours are not spiral patterns. They're more wavy. I'll be tossed right back into Area 51.

"Out of my hands," Annie says. "The Director has requested to see you personally."

Oh shit.

This is way worse.

Chapter 12

Humans use a phrase to describe going into dangerous situations, something about entering a lion's house. It's silly if you actually think about it. Lions are pretty cute and cuddly, not dangerous at all. But humans associate them with danger and have used it in their language. That's how I felt right now, riding in Annie Quinn's car toward the Alien Investigation Bureau headquarters. A feeling of danger and fear.

Into the lion's den.

The A.I.B. has offices all over the country. Obviously, they aren't in the Yellow Pages. My knowledge of this shady government entity has been gained from my time in Area 51 and from my various sources. Okay, I don't have any actual sources. Lonnie and his computers are my sources. From what I've been able to piece together, there's one A.I.B. HQ in every state, with a bunch of satellite offices scattered across the nation. While not as large as the other government agencies, the A.I.B. is easily the most well funded.

This is mostly because of the number of patents they own based on alien technology. Things like microwaves, jet engines, and the McFlurry. The money allows the super secret government agency to stay super secret. Judging from this particular A.I.B. HQ, I'm guessing they've used their money to buy up a bunch of bland office buildings. To the untrained eye, it looks like any other office building in any other city.

To my highly trained alien eyes, I'm able to spot the discreet countermeasures in place. Motion sensors peppered throughout the immaculate landscape. Some hidden as rocks.

Others disguised as plants. I only know this because my old cellmate helped pioneer the technology. If there are cameras, I can't see them. Not the real cameras anyway. There's about half a dozen white dummy cameras planted on the outside of the building. Nobody can get within a mile of this place without being on the A.I.B.'s radar.

As the car gets closer to the building, my chest tightens.

Into the lion's den.

I can't help but scratch my tattoo, even though it doesn't itch. I once mentioned my scratching habit to Alissa. She said it was a nervous tic. I told her I didn't understand what feline insects have to do with my itch. After she was done laughing, she said it was a coping mechanism. I scratch when I'm stressed. It somehow makes me feel better. We don't have psychology on my planet, so it could all be a bunch of BS.

We pull into an underground parking garage, the fluorescent lights doing nothing to keep the darkness away. So far, the A.I.B. hasn't treated me like a fugitive. No cuffs. No stern looks. They didn't even activate the child locks in the backseat. I could have jumped out on the highway. Still, I can't help but succumb to the fear. I do my best not to show it.

"We're here," Quinn says from the front seat.

I'll never understood why humans feel the need to state they've arrived at a place when I can clearly see we've arrived at the place. I mean, the vehicle stopped. I watched us drive into this underground garage.

Instead of voicing my snarky thoughts, I simply nod and continue gazing out of the window.

Quinn turns to me. "I hope you understand, but we'll have to take your weapon."

My tattoo itch worsens. But I comply, handing over the taser. With any luck, they won't inspect it. It looks like a regular human handgun. Not an advanced piece of alien tech.

The SUV pulls into an underground parking garage and for a moment we're plunged into darkness. I turn around to get one last look at the sun. My heart skips a beat when I don't see it.

"Uh, what happened to outside?" I ask.

"Hangar doors close after we arrived," Quinn explains. "It's a security measure to prevent well... you know."

I do know. To prevent beings like me from escaping. Another shudder ripples through my body.

The vehicle pulls into a parking spot next to another dozen black SUVs just like it. Quinn and the driver get out, leaving me in the back wondering how quickly I can hot-wire an SUV.

A knock on the window causes me to jump.

"You coming?" Quinn asks.

I smile, hopefully showing confidence than I feel, and open the door. The tepid air of the garage reminds me of a prison. My prison. Maybe the Director will go easy on me this time. After all, we go way back.

Quinn leads me through a set of double doors flanked by large scary looking men holding rifles that look like they were ripped straight out of that Halo game Lonnie always plays.

"Heya fellas," I say as I walk through the door.

They don't acknowledge me, staying as stoic as statues. It's kind of rude, but I let it slide. I'm too preoccupied with panicking, anyway.

Quinn walks down a long fluorescent hallway. The light seems to emanate from the walls themselves. At the other end is another set of double doors that look like they belong on a space station. They swish open as Quinn approaches.

Standing on the other side is Agent Dunby.

"If it isn't the man of the hour," Dunby says, putting an arm around my shoulder.

Dunby and I also go way back. He doesn't know it, but he was one of my torturers when I was in Area 51. Unlike the other guards, who only seemed to be following orders, Dunby relished in the torture. I'll never forget his stale cigarette breath, as he would tell me how despicable I was. Most people who are brought into the A.I.B. have had their lives changed in some way by extraterrestrials. Whatever happened to Dunby must have been beyond traumatic because this dude hates all things alien.

"Hey Rob," I reply. "Where were you during the junkyard attack?"

"Still processing evidence from the alley," Dunby says, squeezing me tighter. "You know what keeps showing up in these J'kyrick sightings?"

I know the answer, but I don't say it.

"You," Quinn says. "You keep showing up and I'm going to figure out why."

"I'm a bounty hunter," I say, standing up a little bit straighter. Even in Area 51, I didn't want to give Dunby the satisfaction. I'm sure as hell not going to give it to him now. "I'm good at my job, Dunby. Something I'm sure you know nothing about. Maybe instead of bothering me, you should recruit me."

Dunby scoffs, releasing his hold on me. He turns, putting a hand on my chest. Quinn gives me an apologetic look but keeps her distance.

"What are you up to, Ace?" Dunby asks, his nose just inches from mine.

That same familiar scent of tobacco and aftershave.

"You mean right this second?" I ask. "I'd say I'm slowly getting annoyed."

"Funny. I think there's something you're not telling me. I like you, Ace. So I'll give you a choice. Tell me what's going on and I'll go easy on you."

"A choice usually implies more than one option."

"Fine. Don't tell me. But when I find out, I'll make sure you spend the rest of your life in Guantanamo."

"Is that a resort? Sounds like a resort."

Quinn clears her throat. "The Director is waiting."

"Sure," Dunby says, waving a hand. "We're done here."

He doesn't move, forcing me to walk around him. Dunby is an intimidating man. Not because he's strong, but because he's smart. The man has been working around aliens for over half his life. He knows ways to kill just about any ex terrestrial on the planet. In a fair fight, I can probably take him. I'm a tad stronger than the average human. But give Dunby enough prep time and he'll take me down easily.

He's like Batman. In a suit.

So maybe he's like Bruce Wayne.

I don't know. I never finished the movie.

The point I'm trying to make is I should be afraid of Dunby, but I'm not. I know that lack of fear might cause me to do something stupid. So I keep any snarky comments to myself and follow Quinn further into the building. We pass through fairly ordinary cubicles, filled with people who are no doubt using sophisticated technology to track down beings like me. I consider taking a picture to show Lonnie, but I'm sure that's frowned upon.

That brings up a thought.

"You guys didn't confiscate my phone?" I ask Quinn.

She snorts out a laugh. "No need. It's been jammed ever since you entered the parking garage. Only a select few have personal phone privileges inside the building."

"Like the Director?"

Quinn nods. "Like the Director. She's just through here."

Another set of doors open automatically as we approach. The room is much smaller than I anticipated, and it takes me a second to realize we're in an elevator.

"Director's office," Quinn says.

"Uh. Yea, I know." I reply.

"I'm not talking to you."

The elevator begins to rise and it takes me another second to realize Quinn never pressed any buttons. I really am off my game today. Being behind enemy lines has a way of clouding my judgement. I take a deep breath to calm my nerves. The elevator comes to a stop and the doors slide open. Beyond lays one of the nicest offices I've ever seen.

To be fair, all the offices I've seen have been on television.

Behind a large wooden desk sits a thin woman with high cheekbones and short brown hair. She looks older than when I last saw her just a year ago. She's typing something on a computer, the glow of the screen accentuating her sharp features. I can tell the area doesn't suit her, like wearing someone else's shoes. Her actual office, I know, is in Washington. For her to come this far just to talk to me is a little terrifying.

I take another deep breath, willing myself not to just turn around and run. I can do this. She's just a woman. Someone you once called a friend.

I turn to Quinn. "You coming?"

"Nope," she replies then tells the elevator, "Ground floor."

The doors close, leaving me alone with Marisol Garrett, Director of the Alien Investigation Bureau.

"Come on in, Ace," she says, motioning to a plush chair opposite her desk. "Make yourself comfortable. I have soda and those little peanut butter candies you like."

I inch slowly toward the chair. I'm still not sure what to expect, choosing to stay alert rather than complacent.

Marisol chuckles at my discomfort. "There's nothing to worry about. I don't have ninjas on my payroll. Please, sit. And when I said you can make yourself comfortable, I meant you can drop the disguise."

Chapter 13

I've known Marisol for a long time. Like, a very long time. Longer than I've known any other human besides her husband.

She didn't used to scare me so much.

"Ace?" Marisol eyes me questioningly. "You okay?"

I ignore her, checking the corners of the room for any surprises. Despite her previous claim of not having ninjas on her payroll, I still don't trust her. If not a ninja, then probably some gung-ho agent who watched way too many Jackie Chan movies.

"Ace," Marisol says again.

I finally focus on her face. Both of her eyebrows are raised as if waiting for a response.

"You're supposed to be in Washington," I say.

"Yes, but when I heard I've lost two agents, I decided to see what all the ruckus was about."

"I'm sorry," I say before I can stop myself.

Part of me doesn't want to apologize. Those agents would have locked me up the first change they got. Another part of me realizes that all sentient creatures deserve to enjoy life. That includes humans.

"Thank you," Marisol says. "I know how hard it must be for you to say that."

One could interpret a phrase like that as condescending, yet Marisol somehow makes it sound sincere. She knows my past better than most, so I believe her when she says it's hard for me. It is hard, but it's not hard either. Ugh. I think I'm getting soft in my old age.

Time to toughen up and show Marisol I'm not one to be pushed around. Think of something cool to say, Ace.

"What do you want with me?" I ask, my voice croaking because of my dry throat.

Not the tough-guy image I was hoping to portray. Marisol smiles.

"Well, first off, I want you to relax," she says. "You're safe here. Trust me. I had this room constructed with Bekzath technology. No signals get in or out unless I say so."

I nod absently, considering Marisol's words. Bekzaths do make some of the most secure communications satellites in the galaxy. I cautiously slide into the chair across from Marisol's desk.

"What do you really want?" I ask. "Why am I here?"

"Just want to chat. It's been awhile."

I decide to take a risk and drop the disguise, pulling off my hat and wig. My skin tone changes back to its lovely shade of gray. The irises of my eyes expand, heightening my vision just a bit. I take another look in the darkest corners of the office. I don't see anyone else.

It's just Marisol and I.

"There he is," she says. "As much as I hate to admit it, I miss that face."

"That why you wanted to see me? Because you miss me?"

"Yes and no. I really did want to talk to you. To tell you to stop this bounty hunting nonsense."

I can't say I'm surprised. She didn't want me doing this in the first place. I rub the wounds on my torso and think to myself that I probably should have listened to her.

"You trying to shut down all the alien bounty hunters?" I ask. "Or just me?"

"The others are way more experienced. And human."

"Just me then."

The muscles in Marisol's jaw flex. I recognize this reaction. She's trying not to yell. Sometimes when she doesn't get her way, she lashes out. I've noticed a lot of humans do that. Just the fact that she's trying not to yell means maybe this is just a chat. Oddly enough, I appreciate that.

"I don't want you to get hurt," she finally says. "If anybody were to discover who you really are, I can't do anything to protect you."

"Protect me?" I say, harsher than I intend. "You helped keep me imprisoned for years."

"That's not fair," Marisol says softly.

I sag into the chair a little and look away. She's right. Marisol was just doing her job. If anything, she risked her entire career to keep me safe when I escaped. She's risking her career now just by having me in an A.I.B. facility.

"I'm sorry," I say.

Marisol waves a hand dismissively. "You have nothing to be sorry for."

We sit there for a moment in awkward silence. I don't know how to move on from this. I should be mad at this woman. Infuriated. But she is, after all, only human.

"How's Mikey?" I ask, filling the silence.

"How should I know?"

"Uh. He's your husband?" I say.

"We aren't married," Marisol retorts, her face as impassive as ever.

I sigh. “Mikey is one of the good ones. You just let him go?”

“That’s none of your business.”

“Does it have to do with you becoming the Director of the A.I.B. and Mikey trying to expose the A.I.B. to the public?”

Marisol‘s expression changes, only for a second, but it’s enough to tell me I’m right.

“That’s none of your business,” she says again, her eyes narrow.

She smiles, unable to stop herself. I can be annoyingly charming sometimes. Or charmingly annoying. I always confuse the two.

“We used to be close,” I say. “Almost family. Like in those fast car movies.”

“I see you’ve been catching up on current events,” she says, eyebrows raised appreciatively. “I do love those movies.”

I‘m about to tell her that Lonnie introduced me to those films. Despite the main actor coming from a long line of acting extraterrestrials, the movies didn’t really pique my interest. I decide not to mention Lonnie because I still don’t know if this is a trap and the last thing I need is for Lonnie to end up on the A.I.B. Most Wanted List.

“Yea, I caught the movies on some streaming service.”

“There are so many, I can’t keep up.”

“True. So, seriously, what happened between you and Mickey?”

“I already said it’s none of your business. You lost the insight into my private life when you unleashed a plague on this world.”

The comment is lighthearted, not meant to hurt my feelings. It still stings though. Marisol is choosing her tone carefully which, again, I appreciate. She honestly has every right to yell at me. I know what I've done, and it hasn't made her job easier. I decide to keep things upbeat.

"To be clear," I say. "You mean the aliens from Area 51 and not an actual plague, right?"

"Yes."

"Whew! Good! You humans do not take to new pathogens well."

"We have actual alien viruses to deal with. I guess I could have chosen my words more carefully."

I shrug. An actual human shrug. Shoulders moving up and down. The whole shebang. Another sign that I've been on this planet too long.

"So you really just want me here to tell me to back off?"

"That's it," Marisol says, opening her hands. "There is no ulterior motive. When we're done here, you can leave unmolested. I truly just want you to be safe. Oh, and stop getting in our way."

"I think your boy Dunby has it out for me. You might want to give him the same memo."

Marisol snorts, rolling her eyes. "Dunby can be a bit much sometimes, but he's dedicated to the cause. He'll be assigned to another case."

"Wow," I say. "Thanks... I guess."

"I'm not doing it for you. We're spread pretty thin. Budgets cuts and all that. Congress doesn't think we can do what the FBI or CIA can do. Dunby will be tasked with tracking down more escapees before the next congressional hearing."

"Oh. Okay. So I can just go?"

Marisol nods, already turning back to the computer.

"You might want to fix your face," she says, making a circular motion in front of her own face and scrunching her nose. The gesture reminds me of Alissa. The similarities don't end there. The shape of their noses. The small dimple on their right cheek that appears when they smile or frown. The same hazel eyes.

"Have you talked to your daughter?" I ask.

Marisol pauses, her head tilting slightly to the left.

"No," she says. "She's not answering my calls or returning my texts. I'm guessing you've seen her."

I nod.

Marisol takes a breath, composing herself. It could be the lighting, but I'm pretty sure I can see her eyes swelling with tears.

"How is she?" Marisol finally asks as she exhales.

"She's good. Angry. Probably at you. But she's good. You should go see her. I think she'd appreciate it even though she loathes you."

Marisol gives me a tight smile. "You Greymenians don't mince words."

"No we don't."

"Given your upbringing, I'm not surprised."

I ponder that for a moment. "That's fair," I say. "At the very least, you can use one of your satellites to check in on her."

"What makes you think I haven't already? Now shoo. I have work to do."

"That rhymed."

"Get out, Ace."

"I'm going, I'm going. Thanks for not arresting me."

"You're welcome."

I stand and turn to the door. I use the glass of a nearby framed certificate to adjust my wig and hat. Then I inhale, willing my body to change my skin color and facial features until I am, once again, Ace Trakker: Normal Human Man.

I turn to the elevator door, feeling a bit unsteady. I just had a chat with the head lion and walked away unscathed. It's a no-brainer that I won't listen to Marisol. I'll still track down the J'kyrick. She probably knows this. Hell, she probably has a tracking device on me right now. With a prison full of alien engineers at her disposal, I'll never find anything she may have planted on my body. I'll lead her to Jay, Marisol will follow, then she'll finally arrest me.

Nah, she wouldn't do that.

Would she?

Before I can ponder the question further, the lights go out.

Chapter 14

The dark doesn't bother me like it does humans. I've seen humans freak out when the lights are suddenly gone. I usually just adjust my night vision and go on about my business. That being said, right now, I'm a little freaked out.

"I thought you said I could leave."

"You can leave," Marisol replies, standing up. "This isn't us."

She walks around the desk with her arms in front of her. I chuckle and ready myself to make a sarcastic comment when I remember she can't see in the dark like me. I think about letting her bump into something before I swoop in to assist, then think better of it. I want Marisol on my side. Now, more than ever.

"Here, let me help you," I say, grabbing her hand.

"Thank you. This isn't right."

"Could just be a regular ole power outage."

"Unlikely. I had a Faveelin Star installed in every A.I.B. building."

"You know, you're going to get intergalactically sued one of these days."

"I have a Tuulox lawyer on retainer."

"Of course you do."

I begin to guide Marisol to the elevators, but decide against it. They won't work, anyway. I look around, seeing a door that I hope leads to a stairwell. I move us both slowly toward it.

"We need to figure out why the power is out," Marisol says.

"We? I'm leaving."

"The outer doors won't open without the power."

"Well shit. That seems like a pretty severe design flaw."

Marisol snorts a laugh.

Well, there goes that plan. I suppose I can stick around for a few more minutes until they figure everything out. That's me trying to convince myself I have any say in the matter.

"The backup generators should have kicked on by now," Marisol says, reaching for the door handle. She's a good three feet away, so I move her closer. She pulls the door open to an equally black hallway.

"Where are we going?" I whisper.

"Stairs," Marisol replies.

"Duh. I meant after that."

"You've become quite the smartass lately."

"Side effects of living amongst humans."

"Fair enough. We'll head to the control room and see if we can restore the power."

The trek down the hallway is painfully slow. I can see just fine and part of me just wants to leave her here. That wouldn't be right, though. Damn me and this moral code.

A rustling sound pulls me from my thoughts. I squint, seeing another A.I.B. agent at the end of the hallway, arms extended to avoid bumping into something.

"There's another agent down the hall," I whisper to Marisol.

"Who's there?" she calls out.

"Agent Jenkins, ma'am," comes the reply.

Jenkins' features come into focus. He's wearing the same black suit as the other agents. His skin a very human shade of pale like Quinn's. His hair is short and brown like most humans I see.

Human are so bland.

And that's coming from a guy who looks almost exactly like every other member of his species.

"Do you know why the power is out?" Marisol calls out.

"No ma'am," Jenkins replies. "I have Hudson checking it out. Communications are out too. Adams is checking on that."

"Communications?" I whisper to Marisol. "I thought phones didn't work here."

"Your phones don't. Ours work just fine."

"You guys suck, you know that."

"We are aware," Marisol replies. Then to Jenkins, "Once you have the report from Agent Hudson, rally up as many agents as you can and get them to the lobby. I want a full headcount in fifteen minutes. If you run into Agent Quinn along the way, tell her she's to carry out Protocol 14."

"Yes ma—" Agent Jenkins disappears from the hallway.

"What happened?" Marisol asks.

My heart pounds against my chest so hard it hurts. I used to laugh at humans who experienced anxiety. It's unheard of on my planet. The Council heavily regulated all of our emotions. Should anyway suddenly say, shit their pants in fear, the automated system governing the world would quickly administer drugs to calm them down. It didn't even matter where you were. Work. Here are your drugs. Taking a walk. Drugs! Get your drugs here! Getting into a heated debate. BAM! Drugs! Calm down fools! Any heightened emotion resulted in the automatic delivery of drugs either by The Council or a nearby physician.

I wish I had those drugs now.

"We need to get back to your office," I whisper-shout.

"Why? What happened to Jenkins?"

"Gr-green blur. Green blur got him."

"What? Are you on drugs?"

"No, but I wish! Seriously, we need to move."

I guide Marisol back to her office as quickly as her blindness will allow. The door closes with a soft click that's deafening. Marisol releases herself from my grasp, heading to the elevator, more comfortable moving in familiar surroundings.

"The J'kyrick," she says. "How the hell did it get in here?"

"It's crazy strong. Probably just barreled through the wall like the Kool-Aid Man."

Marisol grunts. "We must have spooked it."

"I doubt anything spooks it. It's probably here to kill you all since you shot it with actual rockets."

"Or that," Marisol agrees. "Come help me open this."

I rush to her side, each of us working to get our fingers between the doors. Screams from outside cause us to freeze. Shortly after, gunfire erupts, followed by more screams.

"We need to hurry," Marisol says.

"Yea, no shit."

"You used to be a lot more fun to hang out with."

"That was before I got trapped in a literal horror movie."

Marisol's brow furrows. It lasts only a second but I see it. Even in the darkness, I see it. Marisol is worried. For us. For her agents. For the planet. She has a lot of her plate and I've added my own heaping pile of crap to that plate. I shouldn't have. I realize that now. Unfortunately, it's just moments before we're violently murdered.

I try to think of something to take my mind off of the J'kyrick.

"Hey, how do humans know about the J'kyricks anyway?" I ask. So much for taking my mind off of the deadly green blur.

"They've been in the archives for as long as I can remember."

"No way. We have archives too."

"Yea, most civilizations do," Marisol says, her sarcasm mixed with the grunts. The elevator door opens a little. Just an inch. Then another. My fingers ache, but I ignore the pain.

"Someone encountered a J'kyrick before my time," Marisol continues. "They documented the attack. Some old ship. Vikings I think. The J'kyrick kept stealing their fish. Anyway, one night it got brave and boarded the ship. Killed most of the crew before they managed to fight it off. They drew pretty detailed pictures."

"Wow. They've been here before."

"We've gotten more visitors than you'll ever know."

I think to ask her to elaborate but now isn't the time. If we make it out of this alive, maybe I'll take her to that famous human restaurant, Applebee's, and have tell me all about Earth's alien encounters.

The doors open another inch. I've never pried open an elevator door before, but the TV shows made it look easy. Knowing Marisol, this elevator is probably made from parts of an alien ship.

"Your archives say anything about how to stop one?" Marisol asks. She's sweating hard now. If my fingers ache, I know she's in absolute agony.

"I didn't read them all," I admit.

"Ace Trakker: Professional Slacker," she jokes.

"There's like millions of them. Plus, J'kyricks are supposed to be extinct."

Marisol stops pulling on the elevator door, breathing hard. It's not wide enough for her yet. Luckily, I can contort my body and squeeze through just about anything, but that won't do any good if Marisol can't follow. I pull the doors wider while she catches her breath.

"So how do we kill an extinct alien race that is nigh invisible?" Marisol asks.

"We don't," I reply.

"That's a scary thought."

"Why?"

"Because if we can't stop it, then there's nothing standing between it and humanity."

I ponder that for a moment. It truly is a terrifying thought.

"Okay," I say. "One last pull should do it."

Marisol nods, cracking her knuckles and grabbing the elevator doors again.

"One, two, three!"

We both pull with all our strength, Marisol screaming with the effort; me, grinding my teeth. Finally the doors give, sliding fully open to reveal the elevator shaft.

I look down, seeing nothing but a black abyss. I look up, seeing the same. Reaching out, I grab the elevator cable. It's thinner than I expected and smooth. Aren't most cables this strong braided metal? Again, I don't mention it. Marisol has enough problems on her mind without me mentioning every time she's stolen alien tech.

I pull myself out onto the cable, wrapping my legs around it as tightly as I can. I slide down a few feet, giving Marisol room to grab the cable. She follows, navigating the cable more gracefully than I. She probably has to re-qualify on Elevator Cable Climb every year as a government requirement.

I decide to keep my quips to myself. It's not easy. Being quipping helps with the anxiety. But even I'm smart enough to know when to keep my mouth shut.

Mark my words, as soon as we're out of here safely, it's Quip City, baby!

"Ace," Marisol says. "Why are you moving?"

"Oh sorry," I say. "Lost in my thoughts."

"How can you zone out at a time like this?"

"It's a gift," I say, sliding down the cable as slow as gravity will allow.

Marisols sighs as we descend into darkness.

Chapter 15

I was locked away for many years. Decades even. Endured all kinds of torture that humans disguised as "experiments." Even through all of that, I stayed strong. Now, as we slowly lower ourselves down the elevator shaft, I can't help but feel a twinge of panic. Not because of the darkness. My eyes can adjust for that. It's not even the claustrophobic space. As I've said, I've spent decades locked away.

It's the J'kyrick.

Above us. Below us. Somewhere in this building, dwells an unstoppable killing machine. Humans are fragile. Therefore, they are weak and not meant to be feared. That's what I was always taught on my planet, anyway.

But J'kyricks are another story entirely. My mother wiped them out for a reason. A reason that is becoming increasingly more clear to me as the day goes on.

I look down, seeing Marisol slowly but expertly slide down the elevator cable. She grunts from exertion but doesn't complain.

"You okay?" I whisper.

She looks up at me and only offers a curt nod. A moment later, she reaches the roof of the elevator, dropping down with a sigh. I jump down a second later, my arms burning from the strenuous activity. I'm stronger than most humans. The fact Marisol doesn't complain, or even show any signs of pain, is impressive. Especially at her advanced human age.

Muffled screams and gunfire echo through the shaft. Marisol's face hardens as she bends down to inspect the roof.

"What now?" I whisper. My voice barely heard above the anarchy occurring somewhere in the building.

Marisol stiffens, craning her neck to listen. I halfway expect Jay to crawl down the shaft and maul us to death. After a few minutes, nothing happens and I relax a little.

Marisol's focus returns to the roof of the elevator.

"We have to get this panel open," she says. "Then we drop into the elevator, open the doors, find out the status of my people, and kill this J'kyrick."

"Oh, is that all?" I mock.

"Just shut up and help me. I can't see in the dark."

I drop to my knees, running my fingers along the edge of the panel. I notice a keypad and a spot for what looks like a key.

"Looks like we need a code or a key."

"I have both," Marisol says, reaching into her suit jacket pocket. "But with the power out, the keypad might not work. Try this."

She hands me a small rectangular thing about half the width of a credit card. It's heavy, probably metal. I slide it into the key slot and the panel clicks, opening outward a few inches.

"Violin!" I say in triumph.

"It's viola," Marisol says, lifting the panel door wider. She raises a hand, giving me the after you gesture.

I lean forward, inspecting the interior of the elevator car. There are a few dark spots on the walls and floor. Blood. Human and alien both. Whatever was in here was injured, but it's gone now.

"All clear," I say before dropping into the car. Marisol is a split second behind me, landing smoothly despite wearing a suit and being an old human.

"Impressive," I say.

"What?"

"You jumping down here. It's impressive."

"Why's that?"

"Because you're considered old for a human and you move like a much younger human."

Marisol rolls her eyes. "Never one to mince words, huh."

"What? What'd I say."

"For future reference, it's not considered polite to call human women old."

"Oh. Sorry. I'll add that to my list of Things To Do To Appear More Human."

"Good idea. Here. Help me with this door."

If Marisol notices the blood, she doesn't show it. She probably doesn't want to think about any of it belonging to her human subordinates. We wedge our fingers into the line of the elevator and pull. It opens an inch. Then another.

"Almost there," she grunts.

Just as we prepare a final pull, the lights flicker on and the elevator doors slide open.

"Someone got the power back on," Marisol says.

"Lucky us."

"Not really. The J'kyrick could have done it."

"But it killed the power."

"Yea. Then it likely realized it needs power to let the prisoners out."

"Prisoners? What..."

Then it hits me. The thing I was musing about earlier. Alien prisoners. I don't know why I'm surprised, but I am. Having confirmation that there are, in fact, extraterrestrials being held here unnerves me. So does Marisol's casual use of the word *prisoners.*

"You okay?" Marisol asks.

I snap out of it. Again, there are more important things to worry about at the moment. And of course there are aliens imprisoned here. There are buildings like this all over the country. It shouldn't affect me, but it does. Maybe because I'm the only free alien walking through this building right now.

Well, me and Jay.

"Yea, I'm fine," I say. "Where to now?"

Marisol taps her ear to let me know she's listening to something. Communications must have also been restored. The look on her face tells me whatever she's hearing isn't good.

"We have to get down to the holding cells," Marisol says, her face ashen.

"What happened?" I ask, not sure if I want to know the answer.

"The J'kyrick. It... it attacked the holding cells. Some of my people are hurt."

"I'm sorry," I say.

It's automatic. I'm not even sure if I mean it. But Marisol has been good to me and she deserves a little empathy at the moment.

"Thank you," she replies. "There's more bad news. It also released the prisoners and attacked the Grobelvek."

Despite myself, I gasp.

Not because there are now more alien convicts running around. Because I'm the reason Bogart's here in the first place. If he's dead, that's on me. I didn't become a bounty hunter to kill my own kind. Even indirectly.

"How do we get to the cells?" I ask.

Chapter 16

There's something to be said about government expenditure. I remember hearing human agents at Area 51 joke about it. Five hundred dollars for a toilet seat. One thousand for a hammer. That sort of thing.

Now that the power has returned, I can see the American tax dollars at work. I've seen it all before, of course. But Area 51 is a top secret facility that few even know exists. Scientists can conduct experiments without worrying about prying eyes. Hell, an alien could escape, run for ten miles in any direction, then be apprehended again with no one being none the wiser.

This building, however, is in the middle of a city. The amount of high-tech stuff here is staggering. Marisol punches in a key code and the elevator descends further into the Earth. It goes that way for several minutes and not for the first time; I wonder just deep this rabbit hole goes.

"How did you all do this?" I ask Marisol.

"Do what?"

"Build all this. Dig a hole several stories into the ground to house rogue aliens? I'm sure you needed some permits or something."

Marisol offers a tight smile. "It wasn't easy. Some of the alien technology we've confiscated over the years has helped. We were able to dig 100 times faster using that alone. Once that was done, it was pretty easy to build up from there."

"What happens when an alien escapes?"

"Hasn't happened before. Not until today."

"But what's the plan for if one does?"

"Why are so curious? Thinking about offering some of our secrets to your friends?"

"Forget it," I reply, unable to hide the anger in my voice.

I don't have to be here. I can just walk away. At least that's what Marisol tells me. Descending further into the darkness, I feel like I might become a prisoner again.

"I'm sorry," Marisol says, her voice soft. "I didn't mean that, Ace."

She touches my arm. I try not to flinch.

"I know this is all weird for you," she continues. "I didn't mean to imply you were taking up sides."

"It's okay," I reply."You're right. This is weird. Honestly, I'm not even sure which side I would take up."

"After everything we put you through, I don't blame you."

I give her a small smile. I'm surprised by her honesty. Then again, Marisol has always been honest. Brutally so. I guess I'm more surprised by her sincerity.

The elevator stops, the doors opening to a long hallway. The walls, floor, and ceiling all look to be made of brushed stainless steel with light seemingly coming from nowhere and everywhere. It's cold. Not in the physical sense, although it is chilly. The entire hallway looks like an advertisement for some metal sanitation company.

I've seen igloos with more warmth.

"You guys really need to fire your interior decorator," I say.

Marisol snorts. "It's Cherulian steel. Strongest material on Earth."

"And on Planet Cherulia. Ya know, where it was created."

“Don’t start," she tuts, leading me down the hallway. "Yes, we take alien technology and use it for our own purposes. It’s the only way to keep humans safe.”

“Whatever you say, Director.”

Marisol rolls her eyes and sighs. We‘ve had this argument before. Shortly after I busted out of the big house. I understand where she’s coming from. Doesn’t mean I have to like it.

“Wait,” Marisol says, clutching my arm. “Is that...?”

“Blood,” I reply. “Lots of blood.”

“Shit. Is it...?”

“Human? Yea, as far as I can tell.”

“Damn. I was hoping my people hurt the J’kyrick.”

“I doubt it.”

We move cautiously down the hall. The walls covered with blood splatter and red hand prints. There are even puddles on the floor. The only good news is that Cherulian steel is very easy to clean. Okay, that's a little morbid. Then again, I'm in a metal hallway covered in blood. Only blood.

“No bodies,” I say.

Marisol doesn‘t reply, her face grim. I’ve been so caught up in my own thoughts, I haven’t taken the time to acknowledge how she must be feeling.

We reach the second set of doors. More blood splattered on the surface. Whatever happened here was a massacre.

“Through here,” Marisol says.

She taps the smooth metal next to the door. I don‘t see a keypad, but the surface lights up as it reacts to her touch. A moment later, the door slides open to the holding cells. Glass walls line both sides of the room. There’s at least a dozen cells, all with open doors.

Shadows move in the distance. Marisol walks toward them, showing no fear. If one of those shadows turns out to be Jay, I'm confident Marisol will take him on herself. She might even win. She can be scary sometimes.

"Marisol," I whisper. "Wait. We don't know..."

She's already gone, moving deeper into the jail. The shadows shift, one rising to its feet. It points something at us. At Marisol.

"Stand down," she calls out.

"Director?" a voice says, relief clear in their voice.

"Status report?" Marisol says.

She's all business now, which somehow makes her even scarier.

As I get closer, I see the mass of shadows is actually seven A.I.B. agents and three extraterrestrials. All of them are wounded, some more than others. Only three of the agents can stand on their own. Two are unconscious. The remaining two are scooting around on their butts, applying first aid to their fallen comrades and to the injured aliens.

"Agent Boyd," Marisol addresses the first agent to speak. "What happened here?"

"A J'kyrick, ma'am. Came through the air duct, we think. Tried to hold it off, but it tore through us like tissue paper. Even chased a few others to the elevators. Then it opened the cell doors. I..."

Boyd trails off, his eyes sullen. He looks like he's on the verge of a breakdown. I can't blame him. He looked into the eyes of a J'kyrick and came out alive. Takes a while to process something like that. The only reason I haven't broken down is because of compartmentalization. I can bury my emotions so deep, not even the world's best deep core driller can find them. Who Lonnie tells me is a guy named Harry Stamper.

"Take your time," Marisol tells Boyd. "It's alright now."

Boyd takes a deep breath and does that weird thing humans do when they agree with something. Moves his head up and down, a lot. Like a lot a lot.

"It all happened so fast," Boyd says, "I don't know how the J'kyrick knew how to open the cell doors. But it did. The prisoners escaped. Most ran for the elevators. Some stayed behind to help us. The J'kyrick attacked them. We've been here patching our wounds ever since."

"You did good, Boyd."

"Thank you, ma'am."

"Can you call for help on that thing?" I ask, pointing to Marisol's ear.

She shakes her head. "For internal communication only."

"That's a dumb design."

"We have phones, Ace. I just didn't grab mine in all the excitement."

"That's just dumb."

Marisol sighs as Boyd invades my personal space. Whatever fear he was experiencing a moment ago is now gone. He's back to being a badass A.I.B. agent who feels the need to defend his boss.

"Who the hell are you?" he asks, jabbing a finger into my chest.

I grab the finger and shake it.

"Ace. Nice to meet you."

Boyd gives me a perplexed look as Marisol steps toward us.

"He's on our side," Marisol tells her agents. "Alien bounty hunter. He's been cleared."

Boyd backs away, but not before giving me the stink eye again.

"I have my phone, ma'am," he says, pulling a metal rectangle out of his pocket. "They weren't working before. I didn't think to check again when the power came back on. Been a little busy."

"It's alright. Go ahead and call for help. Code Red. We'll likely need the next closest field office to take up the slack for a while."

"I'm on it, ma'am."

Boyd disappears into the shadows, calling for reinforcements. I need to be out of here before they arrive.

"Where's Bogart?" I ask.

"Who?" another agent answers.

"The Grobelvek," Marisol says. "He needs to speak to the Grobelvek."

"He better make it quick," the agent says. "It's badly injured. The J'kyrick went for it first."

Chapter 17

As I move toward Bogart, I take in the carnage. My legs feel heavy. Not because of Earth's gravity, which is actually very weak compared to other planets. Alissa would say my legs feel heavy because of guilt, to which I would reply, guilt is a human construct. But she would be right. Don't tell her I said that.

Several injured aliens lie on the floor. One looks like a giant centipede. A Gruvlet, perhaps. The other might be a Manigol. I can't tell. Two shapes I can definitely make out are the Grunkels. They're both dead. Both are also here because of me. Both dead because of me. Don't do that to yourself, Ace.

The J'kyrick did this.

I approach Bogart, who's laying on a cot with one hand pressed to his chest. Most of the wound is covered but I see enough to know it's fatal. Bogart doesn't have long. I only have minutes, maybe seconds, to question him.

"Hey," I say. "Remember me?"

Bogart doesn't answer. His eyes are unfocused as he stares at the ceiling. I sit on the edge of the cot, grabbing Bogart's free hand. I'm not sure it does anything, but I've seen humans do it on television. If anything, it will help him focus.

I hope.

"Hey," I say again. "What's your name?"

"Name?" Bogart says in rough English, still staring at the ceiling.

"Yes. Your name. What is it?"

Bogart blinks slowly, then turns to look at me. If he recognizes me, he doesn't show it.

"Too difficult to pronounce," he replies.

"That's understandable," I say. "I've been calling you Bogart."

"Why?"

"Too difficult to explain."

Bogart sighs in what I know in his species means laughter. Well, a slight chuckle. His eyes come back into focus. Just slightly.

"Bounty hunter," he says.

"Yea, that's me. I'm sorry I got you in this mess."

"Prince..."

I flinch in surprise. Had Bogart seen through my disguise? Enough to distinguish who I really am? I don't think that's possible. There's no way he could know that. Not unless someone told him.

"I haven't been called that in a long time," I say.

Bogart smiles, a genuine human smile full of sharp teeth. Honestly, it's terrifying. A second later, his eyes lose focus again. A small part of me is worried he'll lash out in rage. He'd be completely justified. I don't even know if I'd stop him. I'm the reason he's here. Just like I'm the reason so many dangerous aliens got loose in the first place. No matter what I do, it's always seems to be the wrong move.

"Lord J'Nel," Bogart says, then lets out a bloody cough.

"Who?" I ask. "The J'kyrick?"

Bogart gives a human shrug, which I translate as a Grobelvekian nod.

"What about him? And why are you calling him 'Lord'? You know what, forget the last question. I don't even care. Why did he attack you?"

"Device..." Bogart croaks.

"The sphere I saw you give him?"

Another nod.

"You were helping him? You gave him that thing. What does it do?"

"Here..." Bogarts says. "It bring his kind here."

A final cough and Bogart is gone. A range of emotions wash over me. Sadness. Fear. Anger. All mixed together like fruit in a blender. Unlike a smoothie, these emotions leave a nasty taste in my mouth.

"You okay?" a voice asks.

Marisol. I didn't even hear her approach. Too lost in my own thoughts. The sphere will bring Jay's people here. To Earth. Which tells me two things. One: there are more J'kyricks out there. Two: Earth is screwed.

"Ace?"

"Yea. Sorry. I'm fine. Did you hear all of that?"

"I did."

"Any of it mean anything to you?"

"It does not."

"You're a big help."

"Yea, well, I have a lot going on right now. Listen, Ace..."

Marisol pauses as if waiting for something. I think she's doing that thing humans do when they want you to make eye contact. So I do.

"Reinforcements are coming," Marisol continues.

"I know," I say with a sigh.

Part of me expects Marisol to place me under arrest. I should be preparing my escape, but I just want to lie down and close my eyes. It's been a long day.

"You probably shouldn't be here when they arrive," Marisol says.

I'm a little surprised. I don't know what to say so I just say, "thank you."

"Thank *you*," she replies. "You probably saved my life. Look, I know we don't always see eye to eye..."

"You sound like you're about to die."

"It's not me I'm worried about."

"Oh."

So it's me then. I'm the one about to die. Good to know.

"I know you're going to follow the J'kyrick. I... just be careful."

"I didn't know you cared."

"That's not fair," Marisol says with a stern look. "After everything I've done for you."

She's right. That wasn't fair. She said I may have saved her life, but the truth is she saved mine. I owe her a lot. Even if I'm constantly pissed at her.

"I know you don't agree with me taking this position," Marisol says.

"For a human, you're really good at interpreting my feelings."

"Believe it or not," Marisol continues, ignoring me. "I do this to protect you. To protect all of the good extraterrestrials out there just trying to make a life for themselves. I respect you, Ace. Hell, I may even love you. I saw how they mistreated you, and no sentient creature deserves that. So I played the game and made the hard calls so I could get to where I am today. So I can make the easy calls. Like this one. Get out of here. Go find the J'kyrick. I won't stop you. I'll even send some support when

I can. Just... no heroics. You find that thing and you notify me immediately. A.I.B. will take of the rest. Just please be careful, Ace. Please."

Now I'm experiencing an entirely new sensation. Is that... shock? Yea, pretty sure I'm shocked. I don't know how to reply, so I say, "I'm shocked."

I'm a wordsmith, I know.

Marisol opens her mouth to speak then turns away.

"What?" I ask. "What else do you have to say?"

"Nothing. It's stupid."

"I doubt it. Spit it out."

Marisol sighs, then looks me in the eye. "Do you know why Alfredo and I had you video chat with Alissa? When she was a kid?"

I shrug. "I assumed you just wanted to show off your human child."

Marisol snorts out a laugh. "We wanted to show you all the wonders and joys of humanity."

My eyes narrow, processing this information. " I don't get it. You showed me one human child."

"Exactly."

"But.."

Then it hits me. Regardless of the pain and torture a few humans have put me through, there are plenty of good ones out there. Alissa being one of them. Marisol and Alfredo wanted me to see the good in the humanity. The things humans hold most dear. Their children. Even with the terrible things happening on Earth at any given moment, children are innocent. Children are good. Which means humans are good.

"Oh," I say.

Marisol smiles, then pats me on the arm. "Kind of our own secret alien rehabilitation plan."

"So I would see the value in human life and not invade if I ever got the chance."

"And what did you do when you first escaped?"

"Hid in Alissa's basement. Oh my God, you made me soft!"

"You're welcome," Marisol says with a genuine smile, then turns away to help her people.

I'm too stunned to speak. As much as I hate to admit it, her plan worked. As soon as I escaped, I headed for Alissa's house. She was the only human I trusted. The only person I wanted to see. I didn't even think of the original reason I was sent here. I didn't think about contacting my home planet or exacting revenge. I just wanted to be around friends.

Ugh, human emotions are so annoying.

Chapter 18

Marisol assigned two agents to walk me out of the building. Right now, we're all standing in the elevator, none of us speaking. I keep replaying the last few hours over in my head. Jay was bold enough to attack the A.I.B. on their own turf. Was it retaliatory for the earlier incident in the junkyard? Or was the A.I.B. getting too close to finding and stopping Jay?

The Grunkels and Bogart knew about Jay's plan. He killed them so they wouldn't expose his secrets. I suppose that's more than enough incentive to take the fight to the enemy. With them all gone, Jay is free to carry out his plan to... what?... have his people invade Earth?

Given the fact that Jay is so hard to kill, I can't even imagine an entire fleet of J'kyrick here.

And why aren't those assholes dead like I was originally told?

I'll have to phone home and file a complaint. If I make it out of this alive. If Earth makes it out of this alive.

I shudder.

"You okay?" one of the agents asks. I think her name is Givens.

"Yea. Just a little shook up. Crazy day."

"Tell me about it," Maybe-Givens says. "Heard you were in the thick of it with the Director."

This is exactly what I was afraid of. Small talk. Why do humans feel the need to fill the silence with their voices? I like the silence. Let silence reign supreme.

Unfortunately, since I'm pretending to be human, I answer.

"Yup. We were... uh... in the thick of it."

"Boyd said you two have known each other for a while," the other agent says.

I think his name is Hystad. I wasn't really paying attention.

"Yea, we're old friends," I reply. "From back in the day."

"You don't look that old," Maybe-Hystad says.

Damn this beautifully youthful alien skin.

"Family friends. Her family has known my family for years," I lie, hoping it works.

Maybe-Givens and Maybe-Hystad both nod, signalling that I'm in the clear. For now. The elevator doors open to the lobby. The scene beyond fills me with anxiety.

A.I.B. agents are everywhere. Some are interviewing their comrades who were attacked by the J'kyrick. Others are checking their weapons, ready to clear the rest of the building. Several are scanning the walls and floors with something that looks like those long wands humans use to detect metal.

I can't remember what they're called.

Anyway, those wands are what I'm most worried about. The paranoid part of my brain tells me the wands can track extraterrestrial DNA signatures. The non-paranoid part of my brain is telling me to listen to the paranoid part. I lower my eyes, pull up my jacket collar, then realize that I look extra suspicious, so I fix my collar then stand up straight with as much confidence as I can muster as I move through the lobby. A second later, the panic rises again, so I lower my eyes a second time.

I'm a mess. I know.

"Hey Ace!" someone calls out.

If I had a bladder, I would have emptied it. I mean, I have a way to digest food and filter liquids and stuff. It's just not a bladder. It's more like a liver that does all the extra work. Anyway, why am I'm thinking about this stuff???

Get it together, Ace.

Trying not to look even more like an idiot, I turn toward the voice as naturally as I can. Which is to say, I almost trip attempting an about-face.

The source of the voice laughs. Agent Maybe-Givens.

"You sure you okay?" she asks.

"Yea. Just... tired. What's up?"

"Director told us to give you your stuff back. You jetted out of the elevator before we could give it to you."

Maybe-Givens hands me my taser. In all the excitement, I forgot I had relinquished it. I reach out gingerly and take them.

"That's a nice piece you have there." Maybe-Givens says., motioning to the taser. "Sig Sauer MXP. Feels a bit heavy though."

Great. Out of all the A.I.B. agents in the lobby, I get stuck with the gun nut. I suppose it wouldn't matter. In my experience, all humans are gun nuts.

"Uh... yea," I reply. "Modified it a bit to give it some more oompf against those rotten aliens."

Maybe-Givens nods appreciatively, like shooting extraterrestrials is something she can relate to. I clench my jaw. The thought of these humans using aliens as target practice pisses me off. Pain flares from my hands and I realize I'm clenching my taser so tightly it's digging into my skin.

Best not to bleed here.

"Thanks for my stuff," I say quickly and turn away.

Maybe-Givens gives me another weird look before smiling and walking away.

"See ya later, Ace," she calls out as she enters the elevator.

"I hope to hell not," I mutter to myself.

Now I'm standing alone in a lobby full of A.I.B. agents. I rush outside before anyone else flags me down. As soon as I cross the threshold, I take a moment to soak in the sun. I've probably been in the building for a couple of hours, but it feels like I've been living underground for months. I've traveled in starships for years at a time, but we always had access to the sun. Not seeing daylight while hoping a crazed alien lizard doesn't rip you to shreds really puts things in perspective.

I really need to spend more time outside. Maybe even take Lonnie to the park someday. At night, of course. Life is too short to...

My phone chirps.

Whatever was blocking the signal inside the building apparently doesn't extend outside.

I look at my messages. All 27 of them.

This can't be good.

Chapter 19

I need a vacation. Once this is all over, I'm forcing Cabbie to take me to Cancun, for free. Or maybe I'll just leave Earth. Once word of an impending J'kyrick invasion gets out, I'm sure there will be a buttload of alien ships rushing to leave the planet. As much as I hate bringing up my past to other aliens, I can possibly use the family name to get off of this rock.

Sounds like a plan.

My phone chirps again. Another message. I can't bring myself to look at it. Not yet. I want to get further away from the A.I.B. HQ before I read the messages. I don't know if they can remotely tap into my phone or not. Better safe than sorry.

Hey, Cabbie, I call out mentally.

I have you, comes the reply. *Going for a little walk?*

You wouldn't believe the day I've had.

Ace Trakker having a bad day? Inconceivable.

Okay, I know you're being sarcastic, but it still hurts my feelings.

Noted. I'll pick you up three blocks east of your current location.

Got it. Thanks.

I continue to stroll for a block, keeping my head down just in case Marisol sent any undercover agents after me. With everything that happened at HQ, I doubt she has the resources, but I can't bring myself to trust that woman. No matter how far we go back.

Once I feel like I'm a safe distance away and nobody is watching me, I glance at my phone. Most of the messages are from Lonnie, wondering where I've been. The little guy can barely go an hour without hearing from me. Normally, I find it endearing. Today, it's a little much. I skip Lonnie's messages, checking the rest. One is from Alissa asking if I'm okay. She doesn't normally text me, so I'm sure Lonnie put her up to it. Another is from someone who's been trying to reach me about my car's extended warranty. I flag that one. Might need to show it to Cabbie. I'm not sure if quantum tunneling is insurable on Earth. Better safe than sorry.

Speaking of Cabbie, one message is from him, which is strange because Cabbie never contacts me by phone. Why would he? He can just pop into my brain whenever he wants to chat. Thankfully, he rarely ever wants to chat. I read the message again.

CABBIE: *You okay? I just lost you.*

That sends an entirely new twinge of panic through my body. There's hardly anywhere I can go where Cabbie can't find me. Maybe that holding cell in the basement of the A.I.B. has some kind of mind dampening technology. File that one away for later.

Then there's one message that sets off my Trakker-sense.

MYSTERIOUS NUMBER: *We need to talk now. Meet with me.*

I snort a laugh. Fat chance, mystery person. I've already walked into my fair share of traps. I don't plan on walking into more. On the flip side, maybe this is that shadowy figure that's been following me. Since it doesn't appear to be a world ending threat, I'll file that under Things For Future Ace to Worry About.

Cabbie? I call out mentally.

I'm here. You okay?

Not like you to be concerned for my well being.

You're my best paying customer.

Because you're an extortionist.

You call it extortion, I call it business.

Whatever. I'm almost...

My phone chirps again. Another notification. I sigh.

MYSTERIOUS NUMBER: *Please stop avoiding me. Tell your 'cabbie' to bring you to Outlanders Pub. Corner of 173rd and 22nd Ave. Not far from where you are now.*

Well, now I have to reply. Whoever this person is knows I use Cabbie to get around. They also somehow know my location. Lonnie assured me nobody could hack into this phone.

Note to self: Yell at Lonnie, later.

I tap away a quick message while looking at the human passersby. Nobody seems to pay me any attention.

ME: *Who are you?*

MYSTERIOUS NUMBER: *You'll know soon enough. Please hurry.*

ME: *Are you going to steal my kidney?*

MYSTERIOUS NUMBER: *You don't have a kidney. Just get here. Now.*

Welp, whoever this is definitely knows I'm an alien. This should be interesting. I could be walking into a trap. Some black market dealer who sells alien body parts as an aphrodisiac.

Cabbie? I mentally call out again.

Yea, I got it. Be there in a sec.

While I wait for Cabbie to arrive, I think about everything going on. I don't know who the figure is who's been following me but hopefully it's the same person I'm about to meet. That would solve at least one mystery. Unfortunately, still leaves a few other mysteries remaining. Like, I still don't know how J'kyricks survived the extinction level event perpetrated by my mother. I also don't know what the device Jay has actually does. If Bogart is to be believed, it could bring about the end of the human race. And instead of trying to stop Jay, I'm on my way to a blind date.

I really need to work on getting my priorities in order.

Chapter 20

It takes about fifteen minutes to get to Outlanders Pub from where Cabbie picked me up. The mystery texter was right, not far away at all. Cabbie didn't even need to open a quantum tunnel. Which means I get to pay a normal cab fare for once. Even though the pub isn't far from a metropolitan area, it's still somehow located in an area nobody would care to look. Hidden between two tall buildings, Outlanders Pub could be mistaken for the back alley exit to a restaurant or a club. If I were just walking by, I wouldn't have given it a second glance. I'm guessing that's the point.

Cabbie pulls the silver sedan into a parking spot while look around. This particular Cabbie is wearing a cheap smartwatch I gifted him. It has built-in GPS which relays the watch's location to my phone. I was hoping to track him and see what he does when he's not shuffling me around. I still don't fully understand the whole Cabbie hive mind thing.

Do they all meet up somewhere? Do they all have different lives? Are any of them married? With kids? Or dogs?

I'm ashamed to admit, I've spent an unhealthy amount of free time trying to figure out if the Cabbies have down time. From what I gathered, they just drive people around all day and night. There were a few instances where the signal just disappeared. I assumed it was when they were moving through quantum tunnels. I honestly can't be sure.

Sneaky alien hive mind. I'll figure out your secrets. One day.

"No you won't," Cabbie says from the front seat with a grin.

"Get out of my head!"

"See anything out of the ordinary?" Cabbie motions toward the pub.

I take in the scene, soaking up as many details as possible. I'm not familiar with human pubs. From what I've seen on television, they are places where everybody knows your name. Other than that, they don't appear to be too different from places built for leisure on Greymenia. A place where people can go to socialize and eat food or drink liquids that lower inhibitions.

Getting drunk is a universal language.

Several people enter the pub, laughing and chatting away. I don't know how to describe it but they appear to be... natural. Like they aren't pretending to be happy to put on a show. Honestly, nothing looks out of the ordinary. Just humans doing human things. I don't sense any danger. Then Cabbie puts a damper on things, as he does.

"Something doesn't feel right," he says.

"What's wrong?" I ask. "Looks fine to me."

"Yea, it looks fine on the outside. On the inside, I can't sense anyone."

"Wait. You can sense other people besides me?"

"Of course. Did you think you were the only one?"

"Pssh. Nooo," I say.

Cabbie shakes his head. "Be careful in there. If anything goes wrong, you might not be able to contact me."

"Roger that."

I check my taser, making sure it's easily accessible, then open the door saying a quick goodbye to Cabbie. His expression tells me he's still dubious. I can't tell is he genuinely cares or if he's worried about losing a fare.

I rush to the entrance, noticing the dark blue door with the words “Outlanders Pub” painted in bright red. Another sign hangs above the entrance but it's just a weird logo. It kind of resembles a flying saucer. Cute. Real cute. Large windows flank both sides of the door but I can’t see in. A combination of the sun and window tint prevents anyone passing by from snooping.

As I reach for the handle, the door opens to a human looking couple exiting the pub. They‘re just as jovial as the people I saw when I first arrived. Before I can squeeze across the threshold, the door closes quickly. A little too quickly. I place my hand on the handle and pull but the door doesn't budge. I pull a little harder and it finally gives. I swear I heard a faint metallic click. Like a lock being disengaged.

Weird.

Once inside, I notice the change in atmosphere. I don‘t mean the general feeling of the place. I mean the literal atmosphere. The air is thicker inside. The humidity is high. I quite like it. But then again, I’m not an Earthling.

This place is starting to make sense.

“Can I help you?” an overly chipper young hostess asks.

She‘s short, with long brown hair. She looks human but I know better.

“I’m... uh... looking for someone," I say.

“Name?”

“I don’t know.”

The hostess‘s smile doesn’t waver.

"Well, make yourself comfortable and look around for your friend."

She turns to leave.

"Wait," I stop her. "What is this place?"

"Outlanders Pub, of course!" And with that she's gone, disappearing into the back.

Sure, because that definitely answers my question.

I look around, surprised to see that some of the patrons aren't human at all. At least, they aren't wearing any kind of disguise. I see a green skinned Skimurian and a scaly Hy-Gorbuloc. I see at least a dozen other different species as I slowly walk around. There are also several humans, or aliens who decided to remain disguised, having drinks and laughs. It's kind of surreal. A place where aliens can be themselves openly without fear of being caught.

A thought occurs to me. Could any of the aliens I unleashed also be here? If so, should I call in the calvary?

"I wouldn't do that, if I were you?" a voice says to my left.

I turn to see a relatively young looking human (I think) male sitting in a booth. With his close cut brown hair, pale skin, and blue sweater, he looks vaguely familiar.

"Do what?" I ask.

"Do what you were thinking. Calling in reinforcements."

"How did you..."

"Join me for a drink... Ace."

He just did the dramatic pause and name reveal thing to show that he knows who I am. Respect. The countless hours of television I've watched has prepared me for just this moment.

"You have me at a disadvantage," I say. "You know my name, but I don't know yours."

The man sighs. "This isn't some detective noir thriller. I'm the one who's been texting you. Now sit down."

"Oh," I say and slide into the booth. "You could have just led with that."

"I couldn't pass up the chance to do the dramatic pause, name reveal thing."

"I knew it!"

"Look, I'll cut right to the chase. I need your help."

I'm listening, but I'm not paying attention. This man looks so familiar and it's going to drive me crazy until I figure it out.

"...could doom us all," the man says as I tune back in.

"Uh. I didn't get any of that," I say.

He sighs again. Even that seems off. Like it's practiced. Almost like he's trying to simulate being human.

"You're an alien," I whisper.

"I'm not sure why you're whispering," he replies. "But yes. I am. And I need your help."

"Who are you?"

The man looks slightly offended, which also comes across as artificial. "You mean you don't recognize me?"

"Am I supposed to?"

"Let me give you a hint," the man says, then straightens his posture. "Here at FacePlace, we use complex algorithms to match you with people who share similar interests."

I gasp. "You're Matthew Linderman."

"In the flesh."

This day just gets weirder and weirder. I'm sitting across from the richest man in the country.

Who just so happens to be an alien.

Chapter 21

Today will go down as one of the craziest days I've had since crashing on Earth. Honestly, I don't know how I'm holding it together. Once I leave here, I might just go find a private place to freak out and scream into the void. I'd get drunk, but human alcohol is toxic. Maybe I'll task Lonnie with finding something on this planet suitable to get a Greymenian inebriated.

Even though I'm not human, I still get star-struck. If I saw Harrison Ford out in the wild, I'd freak out and ask him to sign my Indiana Jones t-shirt. I'm close to freaking out now. I'm sitting across from one of the richest people on the planet. Who also is an alien. I can't wait to tell Lonnie about this. I can't wait to tell everyone I know about this. Which is only a handful of beings. Even so, this is monumental. I need to get a picture, or Lonnie will never believe this.

"Uh. What are you doing?" Linderman asks, pointing to my phone.

"Taking a picture of you. Don't move."

"I'd appreciate if you didn't."

"I'd appreciate if you didn't ruin my shot."

Linderman exhales sharply through his nose, which I interpret as I sigh.

"Listen, Ace," he says, his voice stern. "You know who I am. You know the technology I possess. I can have that photo scrubbed and your phone bricked in less time than it will take for you to post it to social media. So put. It. Away."

"Sheesh. Fine," I say, rolling my eyes.

I snap a quick picture anyway, then pocket the phone. I'll check it later to see if it's blurry or not. If it's clear, you better believe I'm sending it to Lonnie. Posting it on social media would draw too much attention to myself, so I'll just send it out to all of my extraterrestrial buddies.

"Ace," Linderman says. "I need your help."

"Yea, you mentioned that, but I have questions. Like, a TON of questions."

Linderman sighs again and looks at his watch. He leans back in the booth, muttering something to himself, then shrugs.

"I expected you would have questions," he says. "As much as I admire your need for answers, time is of the essence. I had hoped we could save the questions for later."

"Aww, you admire me."

"That's not what I s—"

"But if you want my help, you need to give me some answers first."

I can see Linderman is getting irritated. The muscles in his jaw flex, which, unlike his previous expressions, seems genuine. Good. Irritated people make mistakes. Maybe Linderman will slip up and reveal his true intentions. Well, he hasn't really revealed any intentions yet. Okay, maybe I can be a little less irritating. Before I can apologize, Linderman speaks up.

"Fine," he says. "What do you want to know?"

Score!

"First, what is this place? I've never even heard of places like this. Where aliens can be themselves."

"Ah," Linderman nods, his expression thoughtful. Once again, back to practiced human expressions. "Outlanders was founded shortly after your arrival, roughly 60 years ago. It's a sort of safe haven slash neutral zone for our kind."

"Neutral zone implies humans know about this place as well."

"You're smarter than you look."

"Gee, thanks. I guess."

"Some humans are aware, yes. High-level members of the government. Whatever agreement they set up with the owner, it works. Rumor is a government agent went rogue and helped to establish this place. Even though they are aware of its existence, the government is not allowed inside."

"Who's the owner?"

"That would be Madame Judith. That's her human name, anyway. Her alien name is a bit hard to pronounce. She's a Skegarian."

"Skegarian?" The name rings a bell. I mull it over for a second and then it hits me. "They're all extinct."

Linderman nods. "All except Judith. She's the last. That's why she established this place. She wanted others like her to feel safe."

A twinge of guilt floods through me. Did my mother end Judith's race like she did the J'kyricks? Man, I hope not. I don't know how many angry extinct alien races I can deal with today.

"What about other humans?" I ask. "You know, regularly humans. Anyone can just walk in here."

"Tell me," Linderman says with a smile. "Did the door stick a little when you tried to open it?"

"Uh," I think back to my arrival. "Yea it did."

"It was scanning your genetic makeup using a little piece of technology I designed. Determines who is an alien and who is human."

"And if it's a human then, what, some alarm rings out, and you all put on your human faces?"

"Exactamundo," he says with zero trace of emotion. "Then we just carry on until they leave."

"Wow. Seems like a close call."

"Nah. Given the location, it's hard to find. Most humans that come through here are allies. Other humans are driven away before they get here. There are sensors a few hundreds meters out. I can't explain the tech, but it alters a human's brainwaves and makes them want to be anywhere other than here. For the few it doesn't work on, like you said, we put on our human faces. But that's rare. It's a good system."

I digest everything Linderman just told me. I could bring my friends here. Lonnie. Alissa. We could all sit down and drink a human beer and eat human food while not pretending to be human. Well, Alissa's not pretending. She is human. But she can be welcomed here without fear or retribution.

I wish I knew this place existed sooner.

"How long have you been on Earth?" I ask.

Linderman smiles, but his eyes are sad. The question upset him or reminded him of something he'd rather forget. There's no faking that.

"A long time," Linderman says. "Even longer than you."

"Why stay here this whole time?"

"Let's just say it's my duty. Plus, I've built a business here. I'm a huge public figure. I can't abandon that."

"You put yourself in that position, though. Why?"

"Information, Ace. Information is power. With FacePlace, I can see what every single human who has my app is doing. I know their likes. Their dislikes. Their fears. Their wildest dreams. Where they travel to. What they eat. It's all there, ripe for the picking."

"Oh. So you're crazy. Cool. That's all you had to say."

Linderman laughs a robotic laugh. Back to being artificial. At least he can pick up on social cues.

"Ace, I'm not crazy," he says. "My species... thrives off of information. Not too unlike your friend, Lonnie."

I nod, processing this information. I only know of a few alien species where information is like currency. I could ask, but I doubt Linderman will tell me.

Worth a shot.

"Who... what the hell are you?"

"Classified."

"That's a human expression."

"Well, I am pretending to be human, after all. Are you done with the questions? I fear time is running out."

I try to think of more but I can't. Not right now. Also, I can tell Linderman is getting impatient. At least that's the act he's currently putting on. I shake my head and motion for him to continue.

"Ace, I understand you're tracking a J'kyrick."

"That made me think of another question."

"No."

"Fine. Yes, I'm hunting a J'kyrick. And in the midst of my hunting, I couldn't help but wonder why J'kyricks are still alive."

"That sounds like you're baiting me into answering a question for you."

"Why are they still alive!?" I shout.

The entire pub goes silent. Multiple eyes are on us. I wave and smile, giving a half-hearted apology to all the patrons I've disturbed. I didn't mean to yell. It just came out. It's been bubbling inside of me for a while until this moment. I wasn't aware of how much this entire situation has rattled me until now.

"I'm sorry," I say to Linderman.

"It's okay," he replies. "I understand this is a lot to take in. The J'kyrick. It's dangerous. I need you to find it and bring the device back to me."

"What is that thing? Sorry, I know that's another question, but a Grobelvek told me it can basically bring a J'kyrick fleet to Earth."

"He wasn't wrong, Ace. I built the thing, so I'm well aware of what it can do."

I'm a little stunned. Not only does Linderman know everything about everything, but he's directly involved in my current case. He built that sphere, and that alone raises about a dozen more questions in my mind.

I settle for, "Why would you build something that can bring murderous aliens to Earth?"

Linderman sighs. This time is seems genuine. "It wasn't designed for that purpose. It was designed to reach out into the cosmos and... well, it's complicated. Let's just say it was only designed to create. Never to destroy."

I hold Linderman's gaze for a few seconds. It's hard for me to tell, but I think he's telling the truth. Call it a gut feeling, or maybe it's just gas. Either way, I believe him.

"How did Jay... the J'kyrick get the device...?" I ask.

A thought occurs to me.

"The break-in," I say. "At FacePlace. I saw it on the news."

"Exactamundo. The J'kyrick burst in. Killed a few of my workers and made off with the device."

"How did it know it was there?"

"Not sure. My security team is still working on that. Ace, we're running out of time. The sooner you find this thing, the sooner we can go back to our normal lives."

I scoff. I don't have the heart to tell him that none of this is normal.

"Okay," I say. "Last question. You're one of the smartest men... aliens on the planet. If you designed that sphere, then how can the J'kyrick use it? If it's as dangerous as you claim it is, then wouldn't there be safeguards in place?

Linderman's eyebrows shoot up in surprise. "Good question. Very insightful coming from you."

"Ouch."

"My guess is, it's been altered in some way. It's not designed to be used by anyone but me. I am the safeguard. Someone hacked it."

"Who has the knowledge to...?"

I freeze.

Flashes of the past 24 hours flash through my mind. The junkyard. The heated conversation with the Grunkles. The assault on A.I.B. and the bloodied bodies of Bogart and the Grunkles.

Jay had the Grunkles alter the device. Then he killed them to cover his own tracks. Ruthless.

"Nevermind," I continue. "I think I just answered my own question."

"Okay," Linderman says, opening his palms in a placating gesture. "So we good?"

"Why me?"

"Excuse me?"

"Why me? You said you have a security team. Why not send them after the J'kyrick?"

Linderman doesn't hesitate, as if he had the response already keyed up.

"Because you've already been on it's trail. You've had two run-ins and somehow survived. You're resourceful and able to get into places my security team might not."

"I'm flattered. But if I do this, then I'll need..."

"Money. Of course. Perhaps you are not that different from the humans. Check your phone."

Just as Linderman finished the sentence, my phone chirps.

I look to see a notification from my bank. Twenty-five thousand dollars has been wired into my account. It's a lot of money. More than I usually make on a job. I'm about to accept the offer until I think about how much money the government payoff for a full-grown J'kyrick would be.

Definitely over twenty-five grand.

As if sensing my thoughts, Linderman says, "There's another twenty-five thousand dollars in it for you upon completion. Plus fifteen thousand for the orb," Linderman says.

"Oh shit," I say, standing quickly. "I better get to work."

Chapter 22

Now that I'm absolutely flush with cash, I have Cabbie tunnel me to Lonnie's place. Hopefully, he'll have some information on the whereabouts of the J'kyrick. The ride is short, so I have little time to compose my thoughts. I still haven't fully recovered from the incident at the A.I.B. then I was immediately thrust into a meeting with Matthew Linderman.

Very surreal day.

Now that I know the genuine threat the J'kyrick poses, there's no doubt in my mind the A.I.B. will bring their full resources down to bear. I just hope I'm far away when they do. I'll likely either get caught in the crossfire or I'll end up being a casualty. Find the J'kyrick, tell Marisol, profit.

In that order.

Just as Cabbie pulls up to Lonnie's storage building, I shoot off a quick text to Marisol.

ACE: Situation bad. Lizard guy plans to bring more lizard guys to Earth.

MARISOL: How do you know?

ACE: Believe it or not, Matthew Linderman told me.

PHONE: MESSAGE NOT SENT

What the hell?

LINDERMAN: Please do not tell anyone about my involvement.

I grit my teeth and take a deep breath. Part of me is impressed. Lonnie built this phone with a level of encryption unheard of on Earth. The fact that Linderman's able to hack it makes him more formidable than I previously thought.

The other part of me is pissed.

ACE: Dude, you hacked my phone?

LINDERMAN: 'Hacked' is such a troglodyte term. I don't need to 'hack' it. I already control it. Do not involve me.

ACE: Fine. Can I have my phone back now? (sends Puss in Boots big eyes gif)

LINDERMAN: (sends Robert Redford slowly nodding as camera zooms in gif)

MARISOL: Ace? How did you come about this info?

ACE: Friends in high places. Just know the threat is real. Can you send help?

MARISOL: Not for a few hours. Lizard guy really a number on the office. We have reinforcements here to help but still coordinating clean up and medical. Will try to pull Annie away.

ACE: Good. Thanks. Will check with Lonnie to see if we can get a bead on the Lizard. Will let you know what I find.

MARISOL: Roger.

I exit the car, making a big show of transferring money into Cabbie's account. He nods appreciatively and drives off without another word. One of these days, I'll have to ask him what he spends the money on. I'm no expert in quantum tunneling, but I have a feeling it doesn't take up nearly as much cash as Cabbie makes me believe.

With all the humans he ferries around, plus the money I pay him, he must be independently wealthy by now.

I glance around the area, taking in the scene like always. Nothing but oblivious humans going on with their oblivious lives. Completely unaware of the threat they're facing. The threat I'm trying to stop.

Something stirs inside of me. I don't know what it is, but it feels odd. Not wrong, necessarily. But definitely odd.

Why am I doing this?

I haven't really given myself time to think about it. Why I'm choosing to help humans? The same humans who have imprisoned me for decades. Tortured me. Studied me. A part of me feels like I should just leave them to their own devices. Let them handle Jay and his friends.

But that wouldn't be fair.

It wasn't the same humans. Most humans don't know extraterrestrials even exist. They had no hand in my imprisonment. Plus, there are good humans. Allies, as Linderman called them. Alissa. Her father. Even Marisol, to a degree.

I may even love you, Marisol had said.

I hate to admit it to myself, but I think I love her too. And Alissa. Even Alissa's father. They're the only humans who showed me kindness in the last 60 years. They took me in when I escaped. Even now, Marisol is risking her position to maintain my secret.

I'm not seeking the J'kyrick to save the world. I'm seeking it out to save my family.

Something moves in my peripheral vision. I turn to face it. Not something. Someone. The same hooded figure from before, standing near the main storage building. He's closer now. So close that if I give chase, I could probably catch him. I decide against it. He'll probably shoot me or something.

He just stands there, glaring at me. At least I think he's glaring at me. I still can't see his face, which is hidden within the shadows of his hood. Deeper shadows than normal. It's got to be some sort of trick. Some kind of tech to hide his face. Or he's just wearing a face mask. Humans are weird like that.

Since the figure is definitely not from the A.I.B., I figure it's one of Linderman's goons, likely sent to make sure I don't just run off with his money.

I flip him off.

He waves.

Again, that wave is familiar. I have a feeling I know this person. Okay, some maybe not one of Linderman's guys. Either way, I don't have time for this.

I turn away from the figure and enter Lonnie's storage unit.

"Lonnie!" I call out. "It's me! I need a new angle on the J'kyrick!"

No answer.

That's strange. Lonnie is usually very good at ridiculing me as soon as I enter his space.

"Yo, Lonnie!" I call out again.

Something doesn't feel right. The room is dark, but that's nothing unusual. Yet, something feels off. A scent hit my nose. Something I've never smelled before, but instinctively know what it is.

Blood.

Lonnie's blood.

I rush to the workstation, the area lit by the computer monitors. There's dark spots of blood sprayed all over the keyboards.

My pulse quickens. My muscles tense. I freeze for a moment, taking in the scene. If the thing that attacked Lonnie is still here, I don't want to be next.

Surely, it would have attacked me when I called out for Lonnie. And there were no signs of forced entry.

I take a risk and call out again.

“Lonnie! Are you okay? If you can’t speak, make a noise. Any kind of noise!”

I freeze again, straining to hear anything.

A few seconds go by and then a thud echoes through the space. Then another.

It‘s coming from the adjoining storage room.

I rush through the hole in the wall and look around. I adjust my pupils to bring in more light, making it easier to navigate the dark space.

There!

Lonnie's laying on the ground, near a freshly dug hole. It looks like he was trying to escape but didn’t make it before whatever it was got to him. He reaches out and I rush over, inspecting the wounds.

There are scratches all over his arms. Likely defensive wounds. Lonnie has tough skin. Very tough skin. Even tougher claws that he uses for tunneling. If he was able to get a punch in, I‘m sure he would have done some damage to his attacker.

“Hey buddy,” I say. “You’re going to be okay.”

He blinks so slowly, for a moment, I think he's unconscious. Then he opens his eyes and points to a hole further away. The hole is larger than the others.

I immediately understand.

Whatever attacked him tunneled its way in here.

"What did this?" I ask, my throat feeling tight.

My eyes fill with tears. Seeing Lonnie like this is breaking my heart. If I lose him, I don't know what I'll do. He didn't deserve any of this.

Lonnie points to his voice box, and I see what he means. It's damaged. A large scratch through Lonnie's carapace continues through his voice box. More gouges reveal themselves as I inspect more of Lonnie's body.

"It's okay, buddy," I say, more to myself than to Lonnie.

I'm this close to losing it. My best friend is probably dying and I feel powerless to help. I don't know the first thing about Lonnie's anatomy. I can't fix him.

But I know someone who might.

"Okay, buddy," I say. "I'm going to get you to Alissa's, okay? She'll patch you right up. You're going to be okay."

Lonnie tries to speak, his voice box sputtering sparks and static.

"Don't speak, bud. I'll get you to Alissa's."

"Cabbie!" I scream.

Already outside, he replies.

I lift Lonnie up, hurrying to the door. I adjust my pupils as we move into the sunlight. I don't care if humans see us. I don't care about anything right now except getting Lonnie the help he needs. Luckily, Cabbie is right in front of the door. I load Lonnie into the back and slide in beside him as Cabbie pulls away. I look around quickly, noticing the strange figure is gone. If he had something to do with this, I'll hunt him down to the ends of the Earth.

If he didn't, then I'll find out whoever did.

Someone will pay for this.

Chapter 23

Cabbie pushes the vehicle harder than I've ever seen before. It actually creaks and groans until the pressure. What normally takes an hour to tunnel to Alissa's takes only forty-five minutes.

Cabbie and Lonnie hardly ever speak to each other. They wouldn't be considered friends, but judging by the way Cabbie is driving, I can tell he cares. I choke back a sob. I appreciate the thought and remind myself to tell Cabbie thank you.

Normally, Cabbie will open up the exit tunnel in an alley or behind a building. Now, he opens it directly in front of Alissa's house. It's risky as hell but, once again, I appreciate the gesture.

We pull up to Alissa's house just as she arrives home. For a second I wonder why she left work in the middle of the day, but the setting sun quickly reminds me it's the day is almost ever.

This has been the longest day ever.

I can see Alissa's befuddled expression through the window. It's not everyday a car exits a quantum tunnel in front of your home.

Cabbie gives her a wave. She tentatively waves back.

I get out of the car, looking around to make sure there aren't any nosy neighbors watching the street. When I'm satisfied the coast is clear, I pull Lonnie out of the back and rush to Alissa's front door.

He hasn't gotten worse since I've found him, but he hasn't gotten better either. He's been unconscious for almost the entire trip and I was so paranoid that I checked his pulse every two minutes. Checking the pulse on one of Lonnie's kind isn't easy. I basically had to put my hand inside of him and no, I don't want to talk about it.

Lonnie's lucky that I love him like a cousin who I find mildly annoying.

"Ace?" Alissa says, following me up the steps. "What's going... oh my God. Is that Lonnie?"

"Yea. We need to get inside quick. He's been attacked."

"Yea. Okay, okay."

Alissa's obviously flustered, but in tense situations, she's a pro. Part of that she gets from her mother. The other part comes from her training as a doctor. Either way, I'm grateful. If Alissa freaks out, then I wouldn't be able to keep myself in check. I'm close to the edge as it is.

Alissa unlocks the door, glancing up and down the street, on the lookout for any passerby. I don't wait for her to fully open the door, pushing myself into the house and laying Lonnie down on the sofa. He looks so small. I mean, he is small. Lonnie's species isn't very large. But he looks even smaller than usual. Frail, even.

Alissa pushes me aside, opening a medical bag and checking Lonnie's vitals. I didn't even see her grab the bag. I'm not sure if I'm able to see Lonnie being worked on. The dam is about to break.

"Ace," Alissa calls out, her voice steady. "What happened?"

"I... I don't know. I showed up, and he was like this. I didn't know what else to do, so I had Cabbie bring us here. Just help him, please. I didn't know what else to do."

I'm rambling now. I know it but I can't stop. If I don't get the information out now, I likely won't anytime in the future. I'm very close to turning into a blubbering mess.

Alissa's voice calms me. "Ace. Ace, just breathe. I'll help Lonnie, but I need your help. Can Lonnie have saline?"

"Saline," I repeat the word.

It takes a moment for it to sink in. I've heard the word before. Several times, in fact. Very popular medical human thing.

"Yes. Saline," I say. "I think his species can handle it."

"Okay, good," Alissa replies, voice still calm. "Can you stand here and hold this bag?"

I hurry to the couch, grabbing the bag of clear fluid Alissa is holding. It's attached to a line leading to one of Lonnie's arms. How she was able to find and insert an IV into an extraterrestrial arm so quickly is beyond me. She's already working on stitching his wounds.

"He's lost a lot of blood," I say.

"I know. But it's not like we can just do a transfusion. Unless you're a galactic donor."

"I'm not sure..."

I trail off as a thought occurs to me. My species is meant to inhabit other worlds. Sometimes even rule them. That's one reason why I can change my physical appearance. It's a way to make myself appear like I'm one of the locals.

"It's worth a shot," I say, pulling my sleeve up.

"Are you serious?" Alissa asks.

"Yea. It's hard to explain, but I think it will work. Take what you need, Doc."

Alissa nods, not pressing the issue further. She finishes stitching and bandaging the wounds, then grabs antibiotics from the medical bag. She stares at them for a few seconds, then puts them back. I'm guessing she's not sure of how Lonnie will react to them

Once he's bandaged up and no longer bleeding everywhere, Alissa gets to work on the transfusion. She sticks me with a needle attached to a tube, attached to another of Lonnie's arms. She raises my arm slightly and I watch as the blood leaves my body and enters Lonnie's.

If he pulls through, I'll have to give him a hard time about having a little bit of me inside of him.

Despite the rage and pain, I snicker.

"You okay?" Alissa asks, eyebrows raised.

"Yea. Just thinking about Lonnie being absolutely pissed that I tainted his blood with mine."

Alissa smiles. "You're a good friend."

"I'm not. I think I'm the reason this happened to him."

"Who did this?"

"I don't know. Multiple suspects on the table but based on the wounds, I'm guessing the J'kyrick.

"Why?" Alissa asks, incredulous. "Why would that thing attack Lonnie?"

"I don't know. But when I find him, I'll ask him."

Chapter 24

Hours pass as more of my life fluid drains into Lonnie's body. Alissa expressed concerns back about me passing out from blood loss. I assured her I'll be okay. My species has evolved to operate with minimal life fluid... blood as humans call it. I'm not sure the exact reason, but my people are what you would call arrogant. We think we own the universe. In the early days, our arrogant ancestors used to pick a lot of fights with species who were a lot bigger than them.

Needless to say, we learned to take a beating.

Three hours go by. I spend the time drifting in and out of sleep. Alissa stays vigilant, checking on Lonnie every ten minutes or so. How she's still aways is beyond me. She murmurs something to herself and gently places a hand on my arm. I sit up straight, thinking something's wrong.

"I'm going to remove the IV," she says, then slowly pulls the needle from my arm. I look at Lonnie, noticing she's already removed his needle.

"Will he be okay?" I ask.

Alissa gives Lonnie another once over, checking his vitals. Well, as best as she can. Even if we could take Lonnie to a human hospital, none of the equipment can actually pick up his vitals.

"I think he's going to be alright," Alissa finally says. "His breathing has normalized. And I think his heartbeat is normal now. It... sounds different. Softer now."

I nod.

"You should get some rest," Alissa continues.

"You go ahead and get to bed," I say with a yawn. "I'll stay down here with him."

"You sure?"

"Yea. Thank you. I don't know how..."

Alissa puts a hand on my shoulder. "No need to thank me. You did the right thing bringing him here. You saved his life."

That does it. This entire time, I've been fighting to control my emotions. Tears now line the corners of my eyes. I didn't want to cry in front of Alissa. She doesn't need to see that. I'm a very ugly crier. Even by human standards, it's not pretty.

"Go ahead and take your face off," Alissa says. "Get comfortable. I have multiple locks and even more guns. You're safe here. Both of you."

I take Alissa's hand, giving it a soft squeeze. She smiles, kisses me on the forehead, then goes upstairs to bed. I remove my wig and let my features relax, changing into my handsome alien self.

"Well, buddy, it's just you and me now," I say to Lonnie's still form. "I'm so sorry I got you into this mess, but I promise I will make it right. You didn't deserve this. I should have warned you. I'm... I'm so sorry."

The tears fully flow now, pouring heavy from my eyes. I don't know how long I've been sobbing, but when I'm done, two of Lonnie's three eyes are staring at me.

"Lonnie?" I say, wiping my face. "You... you're awake."

Lonnie makes odd noises, a series of gargles and clicks. For a second, I think he's choking, then I realized he's speaking to me in his native tongue.

"Lonnie, I... I don't understand."

More gargles. More clicks. It takes me a few agonizing seconds to realize his voice box is busted.

"One sec," I say, fumbling with the voice box.

Wires are hanging out of the torn metal housing. I fumble with a few, tying red to red, green to green. Sparks fly, burning my fingers. Lonnie lifts an arm to help but I slap it away.

"You need your rest," I tell him.

He rolls one of his eyes, but complies, leaning back into the couch.

After a few more minutes of fiddling with the wires, static bursts through the speaker. Lonnie speaks again, testing it out. Only a few words make it through.

Lonnie rolls another eye.

"Hold your horses," I say. "Almost got it. There!"

"You... suck... at this," Lonnie says.

The words are distorted, sounding more robotic than usual. It's the best sound I've heard all day.

"How you feeling?" I ask.

"Like... I've been... torn... open."

I snort out a laugh while fighting back tears.

"I thought I lost you," I say.

"You did. Only for a minute. Where... am I?"

"Remember my human friend, Alissa, I told you about?"

Lonnie's carapace shifts a little to indicate a nod.

"She... save me?" he asks.

"She did, yes."

"Good... human."

I laugh, wiping away more tears. "Yes, she is a very good human."

"J'kyrick... attacked me."

"Yea, I deduced that based on your wounds. I'm a regular Sherlock Holmes."

Lonnie laughs, winces, then closes his eyes. My heart skips a beat, momentarily thinking he might have passed out again. Fortunately, he opens his eyes, locking onto mine once again.

Normally, it's hard for me to read Lonnie's emotions, but today he's wearing them on his sleeve. If he had sleeves.

"Lonnie," I say, gently. "Why did the J'kyrick attack you?"

Lonnie sighs. The sound coming both from him and the voice box, natural and robotic at the same time. Something is troubling Lonnie. Something more than his being attacked.

"Lonnie," I urge.

Another sigh. Then, "J'kyrick... came through... one of my tunnels. Don't know... how it found them. But it did. Forced me to... find location. Optimal location to relay... signal. To space. High vantage point. Clear sky. Has to... align with J'kyrick homeworld."

Understanding dawns on me like the morning sun. Lonnie's species excellent at gathering and controlling digital information. That's why my mother hires them to monitor all digital traffic for any planet we conquer. On my homeworld, for instance, we have a Lonnie to monitor incoming and outgoing flights, planetary communications, and every type of broadcast made. My Lonnie alone can monitor almost all of Earth's internet traffic, but he's capable of doing so much more. Which is ironic because he's considered lazy for his species.

Of course, Jay would seek him out.

I've been underestimating Jay from the beginning. He's smarter than I've been giving him credit for.

"Lonnie," I say, fighting to control my tone. "Where did you send the J'kyrick?"

Chapter 25

"Mount what!?" Marisol shouts over the phone.

I hear people in the background as I pace Alissa's living room. She's still asleep upstairs. I'm grappling with waking her and telling her what Lonnie told me. How would I even explain that? *Hey, Alissa, Lonnie told a murderous lizard alien how to contact it's murderous lizard alien friends and now they're coming to Earth. Better pack because Earth is doomed.*

Yea, I think I'll just keep all of that to myself. If Marisol and I fail to stop Jay, it won't matter anyway.

"Hang on," Marisol says and the background noise lessens as she covers the microphone. A few seconds later, she's shouting at everyone to shut up. Even with the phone covered, I can clearly make out Marisol's voice. She's used that same tone with me many times. Everyone in the room suddenly goes quiet.

When Marisol shouts, people listen.

"Sorry, Ace," she says. "What were you saying?"

"The J'kyrick is heading to Mount Jacinto State Park. It's..."

"I know where it is," Marisol says. "California. Jorge and I once took Alissa there for vacation when she was a kid. Why there?"

"Something to do with the device. The J'kyrick has to be in a certain place on Earth for the signal to reach his planet. Lonnie thinks San Jacinto is the best place."

"Lonnie? You brought Lonnie in on this?"

"I bring him in on all of my cases."

"Ace..." Marisol warns.

I understand the meaning. Marisol grants me a lot of leeway, being an alien bounty hunter who is both an alien and a bounty hunter. The last thing she wants is more of my kind out there hunting... my kind. They have hard enough time keeping tabs on all of the human bounty hunters out there.

"He's just a consultant," I tell her.

"Sure. Anyway, I can have Annie and her team out there in a few hours."

"Umm..."

Marisol sighs. "We don't have a few hours, do we?"

"Nope. According to Lonnie, it's not just a certain position on Earth but also a certain time. And that time is in a little under two hours."

Marisol curses under her breath. I hear her shout a few more orders to the people in the background. She doesn't cover the mic this time, so I have to pull my phone away from my ear to save my eardrums from bursting.

When she returns, her voice is more controlled, but I've known Marisol a long time. I can hear the fear in it.

"Ace, if that J'kyrick reaches his homeworld..."

"I know. I know. I won't let that happen."

"What can you do? I mean, no offense, but what can one Greyme... man... do against a J'kyrick?"

She's right. I've already had multiple run-ins with this thing and I barely came out alive.

"Maybe I can distract it until your people get there," I say.

"Annie and her team are leaving now. They'll be in an... experimental aircraft."

"Experimental?" I scoff. "Just say it's alien tech."

"Fine. It's alien tech. But it hasn't been tested. They'll either get there super fast or they'll explode over California."

"Mari, I can't ask you to put your people in danger."

There's a pause on the other end. For a second, I expect Marisol to start yelling at her people again. When her voice returns, it's low. Almost sad.

"It's been a long time since you've called me Mari."

"Oh. Yea, well. It's been a crazy day."

"Yea, it has. Okay, Ace. Try to distract the J'kyrick. I'm guessing Cabbie can get you there much faster than we can get there."

"Yup."

"I don't suppose he would give us a ride."

"Nope."

It's not that Cabbie has a no human policy. It's just that he has a no humans-who-hunt-and-capture-aliens policy.

Marisol sighs again. "Fine. Where are you? How quickly can you get there?"

"Uh... I'm... nowhere special."

"You're at Alissa's, aren't you?"

"Damn, you're good."

"Ace! What are you doing there? Does she know about the world possibly ending?"

"When is the world not possibly ending?" I ask rhetorically.

"Ace!"

"Sorry. No. I haven't told her. I figured if we failed..."

"I know, I know," Marisol says then goes silent. I picture her closed eyes, clenched jaw, and fire flaring from her nostrils. I hold my breath waiting for her response. When Marisol speaks again, I am once again surprised by how measured she sounds.

"Alissa doesn't need to know," Marisol says. "Just let her live her life. If you... if we fail then you're right. It won't matter. Just don't fail."

The line disconnects and I'm standing in the middle of Alissa's living room pondering my life choices. I agreed to become a fleet commander. I told myself I wanted to help my family colonize new worlds. More like conquer new worlds. Semantics. Then I was imprisoned by humans for decades and now I'm here fighting to save the very people who have made my life a living hell.

What a wild ride this has been.

"You... go stop... J'kyrick?" Lonnie asks.

"Yea," I reply, with as much conviction as I can muster. "I'm going to save the world."

"You sound... lame," Lonnie replies.

"Man, just let me have this!"

Chapter 26

Cabbie is already outside waiting for me. I'm surprised to see it's the same Cabbie that dropped me off earlier. A couple of things give it away. First, he's driving the same car. Second, he wearing the same seashell necklace I once gave him as a gift. I'm also surprised because Cabbie is standing outside of the vehicle.

I've never seen a Cabbie outside of a car before.

"Cabbie?" I say, approaching cautiously. The last few days have been pretty weird. For all I know, this could be an imposter trying to kill me.

"How's Lonnie?" Cabbie asks, his brow furrowed.

I've never seen Cabbie, any Cabbie, worried before. Just another reminder of how stressful these last few days have been.

"He'll be fine," I say. "Have you been waiting out here the whole time?"

He nods. "The others were concerned. They wanted to know about Lonnie."

"The others?"

"The other... well... me."

I can't help but smile. Knowing all the Cabbies care enough about Lonnie means a lot. This also gives me a greater insight into the Cabbies. They're a hive mind, sure, but they have their own thoughts, opinions, and feelings.

And here come the tears again.

"He'll be fine," I say again, looking upward, trying to force the tears back into their ducts.

Cabbie offer a small nod then pauses for a second, as if frozen in place. He's no doubt informing the rest of his hive mind about Lonnie's condition. When he's done, he opens the rear door and motions me inside.

I climb into the backseat, thankful for the few friends I have on this planet.

Cabbie climbs behind the wheel and asks, "where are we going?"

"San Jacinto," I reply. "That's where the J'kyrick will be."

"Fun fact: San Jacinto is roughly 13,000 acres in size." Cabbie says, eying me through the rearview mirror. "Can you be more specific?"

"Oh shit," I say.

Cabbie merely raises his eyebrows. I try to think of any additional information Lonnie may have mentioned.

"Well," I continue. "Lonnie says it will have to be a high point. Are there any mountains or hills?"

"Yes. Quite a few. Still not narrowing it down much."

"What about the highest point? Where's that?"

"San Jacinto Peak. It's about 10,000 feet high. Fun fact: It's known to Native Americans as Aya Kaich, which means smooth cliffs. In 1878..."

"Cabbie, not now!"

"Right. Sorry. So to San Jacinto State Park then?"

"No. You said San Jacinto Peak was the highest point."

Cabbie turns to look at me, his eyes wide. "I can't drive to a mountain!"

This is getting exasperating, and we are running out of time. "Then just tunnel to it," I say, hitting the back of his seat.

"Open up your quantum portal tunnel thingy and get us there. Now!"

Cabbie turns to face me, his face grim. "If I miss, we fly right off the mountain and plunge to our deaths."

"Oh, is that all."

"This isn't funny, Ace. We could die."

"The entire planet could die!" I snap.

Cabbie flinches and I instantly regret my outburst. I'm on edge. I mean how could I not be? I haven't eaten in almost two days, I'm running on very little sleep, and, oh yea, the world is about to end. In any case, none of that is Cabbie's fault. He's just trying to help.

"I'm sorry," I say.

Cabbie nods then faces front again. "It's okay. The end of the world tends to bring out the worst in people."

"This is not me at my worst."

"Kind of hard for me to tell," Cabbie chuckles. "You're like this all the time."

"Hardy har har. So what's the best way to get to San Jacinto Peak."

"Helicopter, but we don't have one of those."

I can't tell if Cabbie means 'we' as in me and him or 'we' as in him and himselves. I don't ask for clarification.

"What do you advise?" I ask.

"Hmm. Give me a moment."

Cabbie closes his eyes, murmuring to himself, rather the other Cabbies. After roughly ten seconds, Cabbie opens his eyes, turning back to me once again.

"We'll do it your way," he says.

"Meaning?"

"Meaning we'll shoot for the peak. There's not a lot of space to open up a tunnel and decelerate, but the others think it should work. But we have to be exact."

I'm not sure if I should be relieved or terrified. I guess it doesn't matter. I'll either die tunneling into a mountain or die trying to stop the J'kyrick. Ah well. I've had a good run.

"Anything I can do?" I ask.

"Just buckle up."

Chapter 27

Multicolor lights flicker through the windows are we tunnel our way to San Jacinto. They look different somehow. I can't put my finger on it, but the lights seem brighter. More vibrant. I imagine this is Cabbie's way of hauling ass.

I check my gear, which isn't much. One souped-up taser, fully charged. A couple of Reese's Pieces covered in lint. A pair of handcuffs which, even if I could get on Jay's wrists, he would likely break anyway. And my winning charm. That's it. That's everything I'm taking into battle.

I should have woken Alissa and asked to borrow some of her guns.

Cabbie goes through the plan again. Much to my surprise, the problem isn't tunneling *into* the mountain, but off of it. We'll exit the tunnel at the top of the peak and, barring any unforeseen vegetation growth, we'll arrive in a small clearing. Once there, Cabbie will apply the breaks before we go tumbling off the side of the clearing's peak. Easy peasy. Cabbie goes into one of his fun facts about how humans go to the clearing to smush faces, but I shut it down. He looks sad, but he'll get over it.

Now we sit in silence as we move closer and closer to San Jacinto. Once Cabbie drops me off, I'll be on my own against Jay. I won't be able to stop him, I know that. Hopefully, I can slow him down or distract him enough to allow Annie and her troops to arrive. When they get there, then I'll leave and let them handle it. I'm sure they won't complain, given what the J'Kyrick did to their headquarters... and their friends.

I shudder at the thought. I'm a little stronger than a human, but the J'Kyrick can still tear through me like he tore through those DEA agents. I shudder again.

"One minute!" Cabbie calls from the front seat.

I take in a deep breath. Time to alien up. This is it. If I can't stop Jay, then this world is doomed. I guess one could argue the world was doomed, anyway. They sent here me to conquer, after all. At least, under Greymenian rule, we would have kept most of the humans alive. Those monuments of my mother aren't going to build themselves.

I should have warned Alissa. Maybe Lonnie will. It won't matter though unless she can somehow get transport off of this planet. Again, hopefully Lonnie will think about that. I don't want him traveling in his condition, but if it means he and Alissa are safe, then so be it.

I reach for my phone, ready to message Alissa, when Cabbie calls out, "Thirty seconds!"

"Dude, why are you yelling? You're like two feet away!"

"I'm nervous!" Cabbie shouts. "Why are you yelling!?"

"I didn't even know I was yelling!"

"Well, you are!"

"Sorry!"

"I'm sorry, too! Hang on!"

The car shudders, pushing me against the seatbelt. If I wasn't buckled in, my head would have hit the ceiling. The multicolor lights flash for a few seconds then disappear, the sight outside of my window now replaced by darkness and trees. I can't see the speedometer but judging by the passing trees, we're moving fast. Very fast. Branches hit the car as

Cabbie maneuvers around the large rocks and thick tree trunks.

"Stop the car!" I scream.

"I'm trying! I think the last jump damaged the brakes!"

The car jerks suddenly to the right and I'm thrown into the driver's side door. It jerks back to the left and my seatbelt saves me from being tossed into the other door.

Cabbie presses a button on the steering wheel and the radio panel opens up, revealing even more buttons. He's murmuring to himselves and pressing buttons. A loud whine emanates from... somewhere, and the car shudders again.

I glance out the window. Judging from the scenery no longer whizzing by at light speed, we appear to be slowing down. I breathe a sigh of relief. Unfortunately, that relief is short lived.

"Hang on!" Cabbie yells.

I brace myself, expecting to hit a rock or a tree. A few seconds later, I'm weightless. It takes my brain a few confusing seconds to realize we're airborne.

We've driven off the edge of the peak.

Chapter 28

I've been weightless before. Countless times. I am a badass interstellar traveler, after all. But I was always in a spaceship traveling through the black void of space. You know space. The place where everything is weightless. Yea, it was easy then. Now I'm on an actual planet being pulled to my death by gravity. I grip the front seat so hard, pain radiates through my forearms. Our dire situation is further revealed through the windshield ahead. We're so high, I can see the tops of trees rushing toward us.

Also, I'm pretty sure an eagle just flipped us off.

Cabbie grunts, straining to maintain control even while we're falling. He's frantically tapping buttons on the console and talking to himselves. He's speaking loud enough for me to hear, but I can't make out anything he's saying. It sounds like mathematical equations in different languages. Some human. Some not.

Suddenly, multicolor lights flicker outside the windows. Cabbie, that crazy son of a Grovetron, is opening a quantum tunnel. In mid air.

I'd shout for joy if I wasn't already screaming in fear. Cabbie joins in and soon we're both screaming as we dive into a tunnel of light.

Time slows as the tunnel engulfs the car. Or at least it seems to slow down. I still don't understand the mechanics of quantum tunneling. The logical part of my brain tells me we're moving at the same speed as when we were falling.

Which worries me because I don't know where, or fast, we'll exit. the tunnel.

As if reading my thoughts, which he sometimes does, Cabbie yells, "Ace, hang on! This is going to be bad!"

We exit the tunnel about fifteen feet above the ground. We're still facing downward; the ground still rushing to meet us.

We hit the ground.

Hard.

The front of the car crumples as we're suddenly thrown forward. I fly into the windshield, my back further cracking the glass. Cabbie, being the smart chauffer he is, stays put due to his seatbelt. The car remains upright for a few seconds, the trunk facing the stars. Then it lurches forward onto the roof. I'm tossed around as the car slides a few meters, eventually coming to rest against a huge tree trunk.

"Ow," I say, trying to orient myself.

"I second that," Cabbie says, rubbing his chest. "We're here. I think."

I glance out the windshield, but I only see dirt and rocks. Cabbie unbuckles and falls to the ceiling. He's a little scratched up but seems to be otherwise unharmed. Careful to avoid the shattered glass, we crawl out of the car. I stand and stretch, ignoring the pain as it blossoms throughout my body. If I survive tonight, I'm sure I'll be in more pain tomorrow.

I wonder if aliens can take ibuprofen.

Cabbie takes in the scenery before turning his attention to the damaged car. It lasts only a moment, but I'm pretty sure I saw... sadness. Maybe Cabbies are more attached to their vehicles than I realized.

"I can't believe that worked," he says.

"That was some damn fine driving. Well, flying. Falling. Whatever, you know what I mean."

Cabbie gives me a faint smile then takes one last look at the car.

"Now what?" he asks.

"Now we find the J'kyrick," I reply. "And hopefully distract him until the A.I.B. gets here."

"Wait. The A.I.B. is coming here?"

"Uh. Yea. You didn't think I was going to do this all alone, did you?"

Cabbie sighs. "Yea, I kind of did. I figured you'd make some heroic last stand and blow up the J'kyrick with a bomb or something."

"Where the hell would I get a bomb?" I ask.

"I don't know! You're a weird guy with weird connections."

"And in this scenario of yours, was I supposed to blow myself up?"

"Yes!" Cabbie yells. "No! I don't know. Maybe."

Cabbie is obviously frazzled. He usually just drops me off and leaves. Now he's stuck without a ride and worried about the government apprehending him. Marisol obviously knows about his existence and while I don't think she would ever track him down, I can see why he's scared.

"It's okay, buddy," I say in as soothing a voice I can muster. "They aren't after you and me. Plus, we both look human, so even if they see you, just pretend to be a hiker or something."

Cabbie nods, his head moving up and down a little too quickly. I can tell he's still not convinced, but he's putting on a brave front. I respect him for that. This is all new for him. Hell, I've never even seen him outside of a vehicle for this long.

"Cabbie," I say with as much assurance as I can muster. "I can do this alone. You call an Uber or something and get back to civilization."

"An Uber?" Cabbie asks incredulously. "As if."

"You just going to walk, then?"

"No, Ace. I'll just get one of the others to pick me up."

"Oh," I say, realizing that thought never occurred to me.

Then another thought pops into my head. One Cabbie picking up another. I've never seen two Cabbies in the same place at once. If the world wasn't about to end, I'd be giddy at the prospect of witnessing such a spectacle.

"I'll just stick with you," Cabbie says. "For now."

"Sounds good," I reply, looking around. "Are we still in the clearing?"

"Uh, no." Cabbie points upward. "We're below it."

Chapter 29

I've been on Earth a long time. Longer than I care to admit. An unintended side effect of my prolonged stay has been caring about humans. Even accepting some as close friends or family. Another side effect is that, because of my close proximity to humans, I find myself doing more human-like gestures. Coming here, part of me hoped I wouldn't lose my true Greymenian identity. I say 'part' because another part of me never really agreed with what my mother has been doing. Sending her children to conquer new worlds. Yes, being locked up at Area 51 sucked. Like, really sucked. But I learned a lot about humans. And I eventually came to care for them. Thanks mostly in part to Marisol and Alfredo sharing their lives with me. And now I don't know what I'd do without Alissa. She's like the human niece I never wanted but have grown to love. Even the thoughts I'm having now are a testament to how much being on this planet has changed me.

Now, where was I? Oh, right. Human gestures. I do them a lot now.

One such gesture I find myself doing more and more is lowering my head, clenching my eyes shut and rubbing the bridge of my nose. Sometimes a sigh may accompany that.

Cabbie isn't well-versed in human gestures. He drives people around sometimes, sure. But his back is always to them and he doesn't really do small talk. So when he asks why I'm rubbing the bridge of my nose and making loud sighing noises, I have to explain.

"I'm frustrated, Cabbie. Frustrated. You know what that means?"

"Of course I do," he scoffs. "I'm not dense. Why are you frustrated?"

"Because we're supposed to be on *top* of that peak."

"We were. For about 30 seconds."

I release another sigh and clench my jaw to keep myself from yelling. "Cabbie, I love you. But it's taking everything in my being to not strangle you right now."

Cabbie's expression doesn't change. "Look, we fell off the cliff, and I saved us. I couldn't drop us at the top of the cliff. We were already heading down. Quantum tunneling doesn't put us in reverse."

"Okay. Okay." I take a deep breath, calming my nerves. "You're right. I'm sorry. It's just, you know, we're trying to prevent the end of the world here."

"I am aware. What's the next move?"

"Get to the top of the peak and try to find the J'Kyrick, I guess."

"That shouldn't be too hard," Cabbie says, his eyes drifting upward.

My skin prickles, anticipating an attack from above. When nothing happens, I turn to follow Cabbie's gaze.

"Oh, crap," I say.

A bright beam of light pulsates as it reaches the upper atmosphere. Every color imaginable bounces off of the surrounding trees and rocks. Even looking at it now, I can see it's getting brighter. There's no way it's not visible for miles. Hell, the astronauts aboard the International Space Station can probably see this.

The A.I.B. will have a hell of a time covering this up.

"We need to get up there," I say. "Now!"

"How?"

"I don't know. Use that weird Cabbie hive brain of yours and find us a trail or something."

Cabbie squints ever so slightly. I recognize it as him giving me a death glare. I know I've been an asshole to my friends lately. If I'm able to stop the J'Kyrick, then I'll work hard to make amends. If not, then they'll just never know how much I love them.

I wave my hands, gesturing for Cabbie to get on with it. He shakes his head, but surprisingly doesn't give me any push back. He closes his eyes and murmurs something to himselves. A moment later, his eyes snap open.

"This way," he says, pointing to wooded area.

Well, it's all wooded.

Cabbie steps past me and pushes some greenery aside, revealing a trail. I follow, looking around for hikers. If we find any humans out here, we'll have to make up a story to keep them away from the light. Thankfully, I haven't seen any.

"How far?" I ask.

"Not far. Maybe a mile."

I nod absently, lost in thought. What are we going to do when we get there? Maybe I can distract Jay while Cabbie grabs the device and smashes it against a rock. Assuming it can even be damaged. It's a perfect sphere made out of who knows what. It might just bounce off a rock and hit me in the face.

Stupid durable alien technology.

Cabbie freezes in place causing me to run into his back.

"What the hell, man?" I say, pushing away.

"Something isn't right," he whispers.

Cabbie turns left. Then right. I catch a glimpse of his face, his brow tightly furrowed. Finally, he looks upward.

"There," he says, pointing.

"Yea, I know. The big ole beam of light."

"No. Not that. That."

I turn to look at where he's pointing. Lights in the distance. Could be any standard plane or helicopter. Yet, something it off. The lights are moving way too fast. My heart skips a beat. For a moment, I think we're too late. Jay's people have arrived.

No, that's not right either.

The lights are relatively small and far off in the distance. Whatever that aircraft is, it's flight path originated from

Then it hits me.

"It's the A.I.B.," I say.

"Too bad they won't survive," Cabbie says, nonchalant as always.

"What are you talking about?"

"I recognize the technology that aircraft is using. It's... similar to my quantum tunneling. I can feel it."

"How can..."

"It's just something we Cabbies can do," he interrupts. "Allows us to build quantum tech without blowing up ourselves or the worlds we're on."

"Sooooo... what are you saying exactly?"

"Whatever technology the A.I.B. is using, it's unstable. They're going to blow up."

Damn.

Marisol warned me about this. I say a short Greymenian prayer for the A.I.B. Before I can finish, another bright light appears in the sky. There's no mistaking this one. The aircraft explodes. Well, part of it anyway. The rest plummets to the ground, disappearing behind the treetops.

The only consolidation is there's no fireball.

"Any survivors?" I ask Cabbie.

"How should I know?"

"You can sense them."

"No. I can sense you. And others like you. Not humans."

Great. We're are an absolutely worthless duo. I tap my hand against my thigh, another very human gesture. Once I realize I do it, I stop. I need a plan. Any plan other than running at a J'kyrick armed with nothing more than a taser.

"Okay," I say to Cabbie. "You have to break your oath and pick up the A.I.B."

"What! I..."

"No time to argue. Head to the crash site. Communicate with the other Cabbies. Send one of them to go pick up any survivors. If you find any weapons, grab those. Then get your ass back here, pronto."

Cabbie stares at me for a few seconds, likely relaying our conversation to himselves.

"Fine," he finally says. "What are you going to do?"

"Run at the J'kyrick armed with nothing more than my taser."

Chapter 30

The trail is steep, but it doesn't slow me down. Unlike humans, I don't get winded easily. Scientists at Area 51 theorized this was because my body processes Earth's oxygen more efficiently than humans. Also, my muscles are pretty dense. I'm not a thick extraterrestrial but I'm strong by human standards. They discovered all of this after forcing me to run for days nonstop on a treadmill. Any time I slowed down, I was shocked. No food. No bathroom breaks. Zero sleep.

Just one of the tortures humans subjected me to.

Why am I rushing to save these assholes, again?

Alissa's face flits into my thoughts. Then her father's. Her mother's. Then countless other humans I've seen over the past year. Men. Women. Children.

All innocent. All unaware of their impending doom.

As much as I didn't deserve the things that happened to me, they definitely don't deserve what's about to happen to them. I push myself harder up the trail. Cabbie said if I follow it, I'll eventually reach the top of the peak. From there, I can find Jay and stop him.

I burst through some brush, sharp branches scratching my skin. I ignore it and look at the sky. The beam of light is closer. Much closer. I continue running. I'd be lying if I said I wasn't afraid. I'm about to get torn apart by a J'kyrick.

I just hope he makes it quick.

Flickers of light bleed through the trees. I'm close now. I force my retinas to shrink, not taking in as much light. I don't want to be totally blind when I face Jay.

Then I see him.

Standing in the open field, eyes skyward, arms extended as if he's summoning a spaceship himself. I stay within the treeline, hoping it provides me with some cover. The device looks larger now, floating in the air, emitting the powerful beam of light. It's spinning quickly while slightly bobbing up and down.

I notice the silence. No animals. No birds or crickets. Even the orb doesn't emit a sound. Just bright. beautiful light.

I draw my taser, turning it to full strength. I take aim. This won't affect Jay. I already know this. I need a new tactic.

I adjust my aim and fire.

A streak of lightning exits the barrel, hitting the orb. It stops spinning and hits the ground with a thud. Jay lowers his gaze and growls.

I hear it, even from several meters away. Jay sniffs the air, then turns to look in my direction. No, not in my direction. He's looking right at me.

Shit.

Jay drops to all fours, covering the distance in seconds. I barely have time to turn and run as he crashes through the treeline, uprooting several trees as he goes. I turn and fire the taser. It hits Jay in the chest, slowing his approach. He shakes it off and keeps coming. I swerve behind a large tree trunk, dodging Jay's claws.

Chunks of bark and wood fly as Jay swings wildly, roaring in anger. I drop to the ground in a roll, missing another swipe. I turn and fire the taser at the back of Jay's head, causing his head to snap forward, slamming his snout into the tree.

"Ha!" I shout.

Jay stops, wipes his snout, then turns to me.

"I'm sorry," I say before turning to run.

Something hard slams into my back, knocking the wind out of me. I can't tell if it's Jay or something he's thrown. Either way, I hit the ground, rolling through rocks and dirt. I force myself to continue rolling, the sounds of Jay's anger spurring me on. When I feel I'm a decent distance away, I get to my feet and fire my taser toward Jay's roars. He leaps out of the way, disappearing behind a boulder.

I've bought myself, maybe, a few seconds.

I can't win this fight. No matter how many times I hit him with the taser. Or throw rocks at him. Or stab him with a branch. I'm going to die out here.

Time for a new tactic.

"Jay!" I call out. "Can you hear me, buddy?"

A low growl emanates from the woods. It echoes off of the trees, making it sound like Jay is all around me. I expand my retinas, bringing in more light. I scan the treeline where I last saw Jay and flinch when a small rodent scampers away. I look upward, making sure Jay isn't planning to dive bomb me. I only see an owl on a branch gazing at me questioningly. Probably wondering if I have any Tootsie Pops.

Something moves out of the corner of my eye. A tail. It quickly disappears behind a tree.

"Jay!" I call out again. "Let's just talk about this!"

I stand in place, moving my head slowing from left to right. Another flicker of movement. Another growl. A quick flash of glowing eyes.

I try to think of something to say. Anything. What can I say to an angry J'kyrick? I'm not really known for my diplomatic skills. That's more of Mom's thing.

Wait.

A memory fights it way to the surface. Something that happened during my first run-in with Jay. Bogart, the Grobelvek, called him Lord. Maybe, just maybe...

"Lord Inell!" I yell.

The growling stops. Large reptilian eyes appear from behind a boulder. Jay is staring at me now. He's not attacking, so that's good.

"Lord Inell!" I say again. "Do you know who I am?"

"Greymenian," Jay rumbles.

"Yes. But not just any Greymenian. I am known as Zell Ita. Prince Zell Ita."

Jay... Inell... whatever his name is, exits the cover of the boulder. He approaches cautiously, his reptilian face a mixture of confusion and intrigue. Not for the first time, I'm astounded at how many expressions are shared across species.

"Prince?" Jay-Inell says. "If you are here, that means..."

"Yes. This planet rightfully belongs to Greymenia."

Jay inches closer. He sniffs the air, no doubt searching for anyone nearby. He probably thinks this is a trap. Hell, I would think this is a trap.

At least I have his attention now.

Maybe I can talk him into stopping the invasion. Perhaps even bribe him with a planet of his own. That means calling Mom, which I definitely don't want to do. But if it means saving this planet, I'll do it.

For now, I just need to keep Jay-Inell talking.

"Look," I say, hands up placatingly. "I just want to talk. Whaddaya say? Just a chat from one royal brat to another."

Chapter 31

If you would have told me a week ago that I'd be sitting in the woods across from a J'kyrick, I would ask what intergalactic substance had you inhaled nasally. Yes, aliens have drugs. We like to get crunk just as much as the next species. No, I can't help you get any.

Let's move on.

Anyway, this entire scenario is surreal.

This entire week has been surreal.

Jay has killed a lot of humans and several aliens just to get here. I was almost one of his victims. Just a few minutes ago, I was almost added to that list. Yet I don't think he's a cold blooded killer. Okay, maybe he's still a killer. There's just something different about him right now. He's clearly intelligent and I'm not getting any psychopath vibes from him. I'm not sure what passes for psychopaths on Jay's homeworld. For all I know, he could be the most levelheaded one out of the bunch.

He's probably an accountant or something.

That thought doesn't make him any less terrifying. The reptilian skin. The long sharp teeth. The yellow eyes. My hearts are beating like crazy. I'm fighting to stay put. My legs jitter in anticipation of a chase.

Calm down, Ace.

Right now, Jay's not a threat. He's being rational. As rational as a murderous six-foot tall lizard can be. Even sitting down to speak with me is a big step. Hopefully, he remains this way until I can figure out what to do next.

"So," I begin. "What brings you to Earth?"

"Small talk," Jay growls. "Is a human trait. It is beneath you."

Okay, not getting off to a great start. On the plush side, Jay speaks excellent English. Of course, he does. He's likely been here as long as I have.

"Yea," I agree. "I've been around humans for a long time now. I know you have too."

He looks away as something crosses his features. It's hard to make out with the reptilian skin and snout. Was that sadness? Shame? Anger?

"It's okay," I tell him. "I know humans... suck. They're selfish. They think they are the center of the universe. And we all know that's not true."

Jay pushes air out through his nose. A snort. A laugh, perhaps? I don't dare ask. He'll likely rip my head off for even insinuating he has a sense of humor.

He turns back to me. "Crashed here. Many years ago. We were outrunning your people. They damaged our ship. My crew was... killed."

"I'm sorry," I say.

Jay suddenly growls, causing me to flinch. I put my hands up in submission.

"Whoa there, big guy," I say. "I know what you're thinking, but I had nothing to do with that."

"Your family ordered the attack on my homeworld. I should kill you where you sit!"

Jay stands, taking a step toward me. I quickly get to my feet, backing away, hands still held high.

"Whoa, buddy," I say. "That was my family. My *family*. Not me. It was way before my time!"

Realization strikes like lightning.

I've been on Earth for almost six decades and I know I'm roughly 90 Earth years old. According to my homeworld's archives, the J'kyrick race was wiped out long before I was born. Which means...

"You've been on this planet for over a hundred years," I say.

Jay stops in place, staring at me. His shoulders slump. Not much. But I notice it.

"I'm... I'm so sorry," I tell him.

Jay's been locked up or hunted his entire time on this planet. Even when I escaped, I wasn't on the run. I could blend in, live a somewhat average life. Jay wasn't so lucky. He's only known the inside of a prison and a constant fear of being recaptured... or killed.

"How did you end up in Area 51?" I ask.

Jay is pacing now, kicking rocks and branches. It's a very human gesture and I almost chuckle at the sight.

"Humans," Jay says. "They imprisoned me. After crash I was... injured. Unconscious. When I awoke I was in room with steel bars. I broke free, but I still injured. They ran tests. Discovered right combination of drugs to subdue. I was... asleep. For long time. Years. I awoke in new cell. New place. Area 51."

Holy crap.

"This entire time, I thought I was the first. That the humans built Area 51 for me. Instead, it sounds like they built it for you."

Jay nods slowly. "It was a worthy prison. Until you came along."

Oops.

"So... you broke out when I escaped?"

"Yes. Me and many others."

"Why did I never see you there before?"

Jay turns, showing a part of his chest. The numbers '57' are burned into his skin. Given how tough that skin is, I shudder thinking about the tool that was used. I scratch my own brand unconsciously. When I finally realize I'm doing it, I stop hoping Jay doesn't notice.

He does.

I sigh, pulling up my sleeve.

"They got me too," I say.

His eyes widen. Just a small bit, but I catch it. "We are not so different," he says.

"I guess not. What do the numbers mean?"

"The humans called it... something like Dark Operations."

"Black Ops?"

"Yes. Yes, that was it. Myself and others were sent to other parts of the planet. Kill enemies of this nation."

"Holy shit," I say. "They turned you into assassins for the U.S. government. How? I mean, you've been kicking everyone's ass this week. How can they control you?"

Jay turns, pointing to a spot on the back of his neck. Given his scaley skin, it takes me a minute to realize it's a scar.

"Explosive device," Jay tells me. "Ready to detonate should I disobey."

"So why didn't they just blow it when you escaped?"

"Because of you. Whatever you did during your escaped changed things. Humans not able to set it off explosive. It allowed me enough time to find the Grunkles. They removed it."

Jay's story forms in my head. The escape. Jay's run in with the Grunkles. It all leads to this moment.

"The Grunkles told you about the orb?" I ask, already knowing the answer.

"Yes. Grunkles say they work with strange man. He had device, orb, to reach out amongst the stars and create worlds. Grunkles say they can change orb for communications between worlds. I forced Grunkles to change orb. To call my homeworld."

Linderman. Son of a— He never told me he worked with the Grunkles. And the orb, what did Jay say, *creates worlds?* In my experience, anything powerful enough to create is also powerful enough to destroy. Did Linderman send me to retrieve a weapon? I'll have to ask him the next time I see him. After a nice punch to the face.x

"And Bogart?" I ask.

Jay cocks his head to the side. I immediately pick up on the gesture.

"Sorry," I say. "The Grobelvek. What was his part in it?"

"He stole the device."

"Wait. I thought you..."

"I am too large. Bogart, as you call him, is more humanoid."

"He still looks like a giant walking fur rug."

Jay shrugs a very human shrug. Another side effect of spending too much time on Earth.

"He was most humanoid alien I could find," Jay tells me.

Makes sense. I'm guessing the heist didn't go as planned. Something caused Bogart to wreck the place. Maybe he was trying to make it look like a smash and grab. Then again, Grobelveks aren't really known for their tact. It's likely he couldn't steal anything quietly. It's not really the Grobelvek way.

"You didn't have to kill him," I say.

Jay is silent for a moment, then, "I had to... ensure my escape from this world. If Grobelvek, if Grunkles, told humans they would come after me. I regret my actions, but I can no longer endure torture at the hands of humans. I just... I just want to go home."

I get it. How could I not empathize? I've been held against my will, tortured by humans. Luckily, I was never forced to kill anyone. My whole life, I've been told J'kyricks were deadly. Maybe they're just misunderstood. This one certainly is. He's not bringing a fleet here to invade Earth.

He's just phoning home.

I'm still mad at Jay, but he's making it really hard to doubt his actions. I was just one bad day from becoming him. One bad hour, really.

Lights flicker from a nearby clearing. For a moment, I think the orb has reactivated. Then I notice the colors. The patterns. It's a quantum tunnel.

Cabbie.

With reinforcements.

Damn, I almost forgot.

A car appears in the clearing, turning sharply and sideswiping a tree before coming to a rest. It appears this

Cabbie learned from the last one's mistake and delivered a near-perfect landing.

Jay turns sharply toward the car, growling.

"Inell!" I call out. "Don't do anything rash!"

Agent Annie Quinn and two members of her team exit the vehicle, weapons drawn. They immediately snap to our direction, guns leveled at Jay.

"You led them here!" Jay roars.

"No! Well, yes! But that was when I thought you were going to kill everyone!"

Jay roars again as he leaps toward the agents. Annie screams an order to fire.

Then all hell breaks loose.

Chapter 32

The three A.I.B. open fire on Jay as I duck behind a tree. The onslaught showers me with splinters. I scream for them to stop, but they can't hear over the noise.

Or they're just ignoring me.

I half crawl, half run to a large rock. Bullets ping off the rock's surface but don't penetrate it. I think I'm safe, for now. I draw my own weapon, my trusty supped up taser and risk a peak around the corner. Jay is running toward the agents, taking whatever they're shooting like a champ. He would have been on them sooner, but the combined force of all those bullets pushed him back a bit. He's strong, but even he can't withstand this barrage for long.

My eyes turn to the agents. If the situation wasn't so dire, I'd laugh at my ability to pick out Annie. Even without seeing her face, she's the largest of the three. Her anger radiates through the armor she's wearing.

An idea forms.

Cabbie! I call out mentally.

I'm here, comes the reply.

I need to...

The ground shakes, knocking me to the ground. A pressure wave covers me me in dirt and chunks of rocks.

"What the hell was that!?" I scream to no one in particular.

Cabbie answers anyway.

That, my friends, was a handheld atomic bomb.

Holy shit.

Yea.

The A.I.B. is not playing around. Knowing Annie's reputation, she'll burn half this forest down to stop Jay. I quickly get to my hands and knees, spending a few seconds searching for my dropped taser. Pain flares throughout my body, but I ignore it. My hand bumps something hard. I breathe a sigh of relief when I realize it's my taser. It's nowhere near as powerful as the weapons the A.I.B. has, but I still feel safer having it.

I survey the scene. Dust floats in the air, making it hard to see. Even with my advanced eyesight. I can't see the three agents or Jay. I do, however, see a crater the size of a tank in the middle of the clearing.

Annie is definitely not playing around.

Where are you? I ask Cabbie.

Running for my life, comes the reply. *You?*

Same. I need to talk to Annie.

Hard to do between the gunfire.

I pause, listening. Cabbie's right. The gunfire is loud but not close. Annie and her team must be chasing Jay. Or the other way around.

I take off in the direction of the noise, wincing as I run. Pretty sure that blast dislodged something in my torso. Again, I ignore the pain. There are more important things happening at the moment. Plus, I should be able to regrow anything lost.

Cabbie! I call out again. *Open a connection to Annie's mind!*

No way! I don't mindlink with humans!

I punch the air in frustration. Sometimes, it's like Cabbie doesn't even want the world to be saved.

You will mindlink with this human! I mind shout. *Now!*

It's not that I don't want to. Which I don't. But I can't. Their brains operate on a different frequency.

I groan, hoping it translates from my mind to Cabbie's. I keep running, the gunfire getting louder. I'm close now. Still no plan, but I'm close.

Is there anything we can do!?

A short pause, then Cabbie says, *we have an idea.*

Whatever it is, do it!

Roger that!

More gunfire followed by several small explosions. I'm very close now. So close, I can follow the fight by the destruction left behind. Trees broken. Craters pocket the landscape. Small little Earth animals scamper in fear away from the skirmish.

They have the right idea.

Another explosion shakes the ground, but I'm able to stay on my feet. I round a couple of broken trees and soon I'm witnessing the full scale battle. Annie and her team are firing skyward. I look up, noticing a silhouette jumping from tree to tree. A loud crack rings out, then a broken tree truck soars from above.

"Move!" Annie calls out to her team before jumping out of the way.

One agent isn't so fast, and the broken tree trunk smashes into them. Annie and the other agent don't flinch. Don't even check on their fallen teammate. I soon understand why. The fallen agent gets to their feet, shakes off some splinters, then resumes firing into the treetops.

The armor. It's protecting them. Probably how they survived the aircraft crash. Now that I know this, Jay does, too.

He'll keep testing them by throwing large rocks or tree trunks until he finds a weakness.

And when he does, they're dead.

"Annie!" I scream. "Stop shooting!"

Again, she doesn't hear me or doesn't want to. She doesn't even look my way. None of them do.

"I'm trying to save your lives, you idiots!"

One of the agents pauses for a second then looks in my direction.

I throw my hands up in frustration. "Oh, so you *can* hear me! Annie, stop ignoring me!"

"Ace!" Annie's voice says, amplified by the armor's speakers. "You did your job! Leave the area now! Before you get hurt!

The fact that Annie can shoot her weapon, dodge woodland projectiles, and hold a conversation with me is impressive. I remind myself to bring it up to Marisol. Maybe she can note it on Annie's next performance review.

First, I have to get her out of here alive.

"Annie!" I shout. "I'm trying to save your life!"

"And I'm trying to save yours, jackass!" she says. "Now get out of here!"

She dodges another tree trunk and returns fire. Even through the tinted face mask, I can tell she's getting frustrated. I can't really blame her. She's trying to stop a deadly alien, all while another alien is annoying her. Annie makes a motion with his hands to her other teammates. They nod in unison, one providing covering fire with Annie while the other removes pieces of their armor from their body. They take a knee, assembling the pieces on the ground at their feet.

"Annie! Please!" I cry out. "It... he... just wants to go home!"

"I'll send it to hell!"

Humans always have to say something badass when faced with death. I respect that.

"Ready, ma'am!" The kneeling agent says.

Whatever they were assembling, it's now complete and looks suspiciously like a rocket launcher.

Cabbie, I call out. *Whatever you're going to do, do it now!*

A sudden, sharp pain rises behind my eyes.

I drop to my knees as the voices of a thousand Cabbies fill my mind.

Chapter 33

Once Cabbie invading my thoughts is bad enough. A thousand Cabbies is... well let's just say I'm not having a great time.

My head feels like it's splitting apart. I push on my temples in a futile attempt to keep my head together. It's not actually splitting open, but I can't think of anything else to do. The pain is agonizing. I feel my lungs contract as I scream but I can't hear my own voice.

Only Cabbie's voice fills my mind.

Slowly, the pain subsides as the voices become more clear. I can hear them all just as clearing as if they were standing right next to. I instinctively know how many Cabbies are on this Earth and what each of them is doing at this precise moment. The feeling is indescribable. I feel free from the constraints of my own body. The intelligence of a thousand individuals readily available with just a thought.

This is what it's like to be part of a hive mind. It's beautiful.

I feel something else hear. Something that doesn't belong. It takes me only a millisecond to realize it's me. I'm an intruder in this sacred space. And there's another.

Annie.

I hear screaming in the distance. No, not in the distance. In my mind. I can also see what she sees.

There, directly in front of her, stands the J'kyrick. He's confused, eying the screaming agent quizzically. The other two agents aren't screaming. They aren't even moving. Just laying on the ground. My newfound knowledge tells me why. Cabbie used his... their... mental abilities to knock them out.

I'm seeing everything much clearer but Annie is still having trouble. I need to talk to her. Show her what I know. I can't do when she's screaming in pain.

Cabbie! I call out. *Tone it down!*

Sorry! A thousand Cabbies reply. *We had to use many of the Cabbies to alter some frequencies for human communication.*

Just tone it down. You're killing Annie!

Right. Sorry.

The voices diminish one by one, blinking out of existence like dying stars. Soon, there's only one voice. One Cabbie.

We have a problem, he says, and I immediately know what he means.

I see through Annie's eyes. Through the pain, she's managed to keep one eye open. That eye is on Jay. He's advancing slowly, claws extended and ready to strike.

"Inell!" I scream. "Don't!"

Jay pauses mid swipe. I can feel Annie's mind clearing. She's no longer in pain. She's confused, sure, but she's trying hard not to show it. Jay's hesitation gives Annie time to grab the rocket launcher.

She points it directly at Jay's face.

Jay turns to me with a look that I swear says, *look what you did.*

At this distance, she'll kill them both. I don't think she cares. Killing yourself while stopping a deadly alien species from invading your planet is a good way to go. I have to put an end to this.

Annie, I say mentally.

She flinches, causing Jay to growl. I hold out a hand, telling Jay to calm down.

What the hell is this? Annie asks.

She doesn't take her aim off Jay. Again, I'm impressed by her stoic professionalism. Jay backs away slowly, inching toward the cover of a nearby treeline. He growls, eyes flicking back and forth between Annie and I.

This is a mindshare, I say.

Mindlink, Cabbie corrects. *Fun fact...*

Not now, Cabbie!

Sorry.

Someone better start explaining to me what the hell is going on, Annie says.

My friend Cabbie, I explain. *The one who brought you here. He can do this mindshare... mindlink thing. I asked him to so I can talk to you.*

Then talk. Because I'm a few seconds from making this entire forest a crater the size of DisneyWorld.

Oh wow, I say. *Okay, look, the J'kyrick just wants to go home. That's it. He's not calling in an invasion.*

Ace, I can't take that chance, Annie growls. Even mentally, I can make out the tremors in her voice.

I know you're scared, Annie. I am too. But the J'kyrick is not your enemy.

He's killed people, Ace! Friends of mine! Now he's threatening this planet! I'm doing my job. Now shut this mindlink down, run as fast as you can away from here before this entire area becomes a fireball.

No.

Ace! This isn't a request!

Annie! Listen to me! If you do this, there is nothing stopping a fleet of J'kyricks from taking over Earth. He just wants to go home. He'll get on the ships and leave.

"Inell," I say to Jay. "Tell her!"

He stops growling long enough to give me another quizzical look. Silly me. I forgot Jay's not in on the mindshare.

Mindlink!

Shut up, Cabbie!

"Inell," I address Jay again. "Tell this nice pissed off government agent lady that you just want to go hope. That when your ship arrives, you'll just board it and leave."

Jay emits a low hissing sound in Annie's direction.

"No!" I say. "No. Annie will not hurt you. Right Annie?"

Annie returns the hiss, almost matching Jay's intensity.

"Geez, what is it with you two?" I say. "Annie, please lower the rocket launcher. Inell, please do whatever it is you can do to make yourself look less like a killing machine."

Neither of them back down. The tension is palpable. Even the woodland creatures can sense it. The birds chirping. A fox runs by, then stops to stare at us with a look that says, *you bipedals are crazy.*

I can only think of one thing left to do.

I pull off my wig, force my face to contort to its original structure, and return my skin back to its lovely shade of grey.

"Annie!" I say. "Look at me."

She does. For only a second at first. She doesn't want to take her attention away from Jay. But that second was enough.

For the first time since knowing her, Agent Annie Quinn appears to be shocked.

Chapter 34

My hearts pound in my chest and lower abdomen. Right now, it's not because the fate of the world hangs in the balance. Nor is it because Jay is about to tear Annie apart. My heart is pounding because now I'm worried Annie is going to tear *me* apart.

We've known each other for the better part of a year. While I wouldn't consider us friends, we're friendly enough. I truly believe Annie has my best interests in mind when she thought I was just a lowly bounty hunter.

Now that she knows I'm much more than that, will she arrest me or shoot me? Or both? I'm gonna go with both.

"Ace," Annie whispers. "What the hell..."

She drops the rocket launcher. It falls to the ground with a heavy thud, indicating it was weightier than I previously thought.

I take a step toward Annie. Tentatively, hands raised. Annie's helmet sways back and forth, her disbelief evident even without being able to see her face.

"Annie," I say, putting on my best calm human tone. "I'm sorry to drop this on you like this."

"What the hell?" she says again, this time more forcefully.

"This is me, Annie. This is me."

"This entire time," she says more to herself.

For a moment, Jay is forgotten. I keep a visual on him out of the corner of my eye. He's still backing away slowly, but keeps his eyes locked on Annie and me.

"Yes, Annie. The entire time."

Annie rushes toward me. Probably to give me a hug. Not quite what I expected but I *did* just share my deepest darkest secret with her. I'm sure she's so moved by my vulnerability that she's willing to display some of her own.

She punches me in the face.

"Ow!" I say, rubbing my cheek.

"You lying piece of shit!" Annie screams.

She pokes me in the chest. It hurts almost as much as my face. I don't know if her strength is augmented by the armor of if she's naturally just that strong. Either way, I don't think I can take another punch like that and remain conscious.

"Annie, listen..."

"No, you listen! I have spent most of my adult life fighting to protect this planet from things like you!"

I flinch. "Things? That's what you think of me?"

Her shoulders sag a bit and she takes a step back. A few uncomfortable seconds go by then Annie removes her helmet. The anger I thought I would see is now gone. Annie just stares at me. The mindlink we share tells me she's... remorseful.

"I'm... I'm sorry, Ace. I didn't mean that."

"I'm not dangerous," is all I can manage to say. I'm not even sure if I believe it. I was sent here to conquer, after all. Right now, I just need Annie to not see me as a threat.

"It's okay," I say. "Look, you've trusted me for the past year. This doesn't change anything. I'm still the same Ace."

"Is that even your real name?" Annie asks. "Who am I kidding, of course it's not."

"It's Zell Ita," I say softly.

Annie sighs. "Does the Director know about this?"

I wonder if I should tell her. Probably not. The last thing Marisol needs is Annie Quinn tearing through the A.I.B. in a fit of rage.

I just shake my head. She'll know when Marisol wants her to know.

"Ace..." Annie's voice trails off.

She's at a loss for words. She's processing a lot right now. Her attention isn't on the Jay anymore, which is good. I take a quick look in his direction. He's half hidden in shadows. He widens his eyes and leans his head forward just a bit. A very human way of telling me to hurry the hell up.

"I'm sorry," I say, turning back to Annie. "I know this is a lot to take in."

She snorts out a laugh.

"But," I continue. "You have to trust me. The J'kyrick doesn't want to invade us. At least I don't think he does. He was tortured in Area 51... just like me."

Annie looks at me again, eyes wide. "You were at Area 51?"

"I was."

"Oh my God. I'm sorry."

I blink in surprise. "Thank you," is all I can manage to say.

A few more moments pass as we stand in silence. Neither of us knows what else to say. At least she and Jay aren't trying to kill each other anymore.

One of her agents groan.

"They going to be okay?" Annie asks.

They'll be fine, Cabbie answers. *I merely knocked them unconscious.*

"That's going to take some getting used to," Annie says, pointing at her head.

"You never get used to it," I say with a smile.

Annie shakes her head but I can see the small smile on her lips.

“So what now?” she asks.

“Well," I say, dragging out the word. "I have an idea, but I don’t think you’re going to like it.”

Chapter 35

"You wanna do what!?" Annie screams.

I wince. Her voice, combined with the emotions seeping in through the mindlink is a little overwhelming. She's scared. Not outwardly because she's a pro, but scared nonetheless. I get it. If my plan fails, the whole world dies. I'm putting my trust in a creature that has killed people and aliens. He even tried to kill me.

Yet, one could argue, did mankind make it that way? Humans forced Jay to kill. Since he's been on Earth, that's all he's known.

It's not his fault.

"I want to turn the device on again," I say with an air of nonchalance. Maybe my chill demeanor will put her at ease.

She exhales sharply through her nose, then kicks a boulder. I'm pretty sure I see it crack.

Annie turns back to me. "Ace, you know I can't take that chance. The entire world is at stake."

"I know. How about this? *If* we're invaded by J'kyricks, just blame it on me."

"That's not funny."

"Sorry. You're right. Look at Jay. Look at him. He's just standing there. He could have killed you by now, but he hasn't. Look at what a good boy he's being."

Annie and I both look at Jay and I swear he's actually wagging his tail.

I stifle an tiny *aww*.

"He's a killer," Annie says, more to herself. I'm getting through to her. The mindlink reveals that. I don't mention it though. I need her to come to this conclusion on her own. "He tore through the A.I.B. like it was nothing. He's killed... a lot of people. I just can't..."

"Let me ask you something," I say. "What if it were you?"

"What?" Annie asks, her brow furrowed.

"What if it were you?" I ask again. "What if you were imprisoned and tortured for years. Decades, even. Do you think you would want to go home?"

"Of course, but..."

"Decades," I say, cutting her off. "We've been here for decades. And most of that time was spent imprisoned and tortured. And in Jay's case... forced to kill."

A small gasp escapes Annie's lips. It's subtle, but I hear it. Jay lowers his head in shame. At least it looks like shame. For all I know, he could have found a unique looking bug. Either way, the effect works.

"I didn't know," Annie whispers. "I had heard rumors, but... I didn't know."

"I know, Annie," I say. "Jay is a killer, yes. But we don't know anything about his kind. My homeworld believes they're all extinct. He might not have been a killer when he arrived here."

"He was turned into one," Annie says.

"Maybe. We don't know. But I think we owe it to him to let him try to get him home."

"Ace..."

"Annie, please. We're connected right now through this mindshare."

Mindlink.

"Thanks, Cabbie. This mindlink. You can hear my thoughts, but you can also feel what I feel. Just a little bit."

Annie stares at me, but I can tell she understands. She may not feel every emotion swirling through my body right now, but she can sense I'm sincere.

Her eyes water, no doubt because of my own emotions. Annie blinks the tears away, then screams in frustration before kicking a nearby tree. It topples over. I make a mental note to never piss her off.

Well, anymore than I already have.

"Okay, Ace," she says. "Turn it on."

Jay perks up, looking at us both with wide eyes. His tail is wagging quickly now. He's kind of cute.

Okay, no he's not. But he could be with the right TikTok filter.

Annie turns to Jay. "You better not double cross me."

"I will not," Jay grumbles, then disappears into the woods on all fours.

"Ace," Annie says, rubbing her eyes. "Don't make me regret this."

"I can't promise that."

"Ace!"

"Okay, okay. Just kidding."

A moment later, a bright beam of light explodes from the treetops, shining into the atmosphere. Annie and I exchange a glance, then run toward the source. We reach it a few minutes later to discover Jay standing in the same pose as before. Arms outstretched, eyes to the sky. Almost in reverence to what's happening.

The orbs spins in place, pulsating with brilliant colors. It would be beautiful if the implications weren‘t so dire.

This could be the end of the world.

And I could be the reason for it.

“How long do we have to wait?” Annie asks.

“No idea. Hang on. Jay! Hey Jay! Sorry. Inell! How long do we have to wait!?”

Jay‘s eyes drop to mine. He snarls, which I quickly pick up on him being irritated. He still might run over here and rip me apart. At least I’ll annoy the hell out of him as he does so.

“That is unknown, Prince Zell Ita,” Jay says. “My race is capable of interstellar travel. We have developed quantum drives. I do not think it will take long.”

“Prince?” Annie asks, raising an eyebrow.

“It’s nothing," I wave the comment away. "I’ll explain later.”

I won‘t explain later. If I had my way, I will never speak of it again.

Ace? Cabbie‘s voice pops into my head.

I look at Annie. She‘s still staring at Jay and the device, giving no indication that she's heard Cabbie.

I have severed her connection, Cabbie says, helpfully.

Okay, good. I reply. *What‘s up?*

Picking up something approaching Earth. It's big.

How big?

Really big.

Oh shit.

“Annie,” I say, forcing myself to sound calm. “I think they’re on their way.”

“What? How do you know that?”

“I just do. Be ready.”

Jay roars, causing us both to tense. We quickly realize he's not roaring at us. His head is still tilted upward toward the sky. He must be able to sense the ship like Cabbie. I look up. I was wrong. Jay can't sense the ship.

He can see it.

Several flashing lights appear in the clouds. More than several, actually. More than I can even count. They get larger as the craft descends. If I had to guess, I'd say this ship is 80 qizarks wide. Translated to Earth metrics, it's roughly about 10 acres.

Cabbie wasn't lying.

That ship is [bleep]–ing big.

Chapter 36

More of the ship comes into focus as it slowly descends. I can make out certain details, I couldn't before. It's not as streamlined as most ships I've seen, but it's still an impressive sight. Even the little forest animals are staring upward. As it gets closer, I can see why it's not streamlined. This isn't an original ship. meaning it wasn't built all at once for one particular purpose. This ship has been pieced together, in some places haphazardly, from a lot of different spare parts. I can even make out the hull identifications of much smaller ships. It wasn't designed to be pretty. It was built to be functional.

This tells me one thing for certain: The J'kyrick's are resilient.

No wonder Mom couldn't wipe them out. These things are equivalent to Earth's cockroaches. I swallow, struggling to hide my fear. If dear old Mom couldn't kill these things, then what hope do we have? I hope I'm right. If I'm not, then we can't win this fight. We haven't even been able to stop Jay. What will we do against a hundred of his kind? A thousand?

"Ace..." Annie whispers, her eyes glued to the ship.

I've never seen Annie scared before. It's actually upsetting. Knowing that this human, the strongest human I know, is terrified because of something I've done.

"It will be okay," I say.

"The A.I.B. are going to have a field day covering this one up," she says.

She's not wrong. This ship is massive, likely seen for miles. I don't envy what Marisol has to do to keep this planet safe and unaware.

"Just tell everyone it's a giant weather balloon," I say. "That's what they did with me."

Annie turns to glare at me. Her eyes somehow even wider as she looks me over.

"What?" I ask, suddenly self-conscious.

"You're that alien? The Roswell one?"

"One and the same," I say, taking a bow.

"Oh, we are so going to have a chat later."

"I figured."

The ship stops, hovering several meters from the ground. Jay only stares at the newly arrived spacecraft. I can't make out his expression but if I had to guess, I'd say he's smiling.

I can't decide if that's good or bad.

A piece of the ship suddenly breaks away. A landing pod of some kind. It's rectangular and roughly the size of a shipping container. It hovers for a moment before landing on the far side of the clearing.

I hold my breath.

I'm standing by to get you out of there, Cabbie says.

Thanks, I say. *But I'll be fine.*

Ever the optimist, he retorts.

A door on the side of the pod opens. Three enormous shadows, larger than even Jay, slowly stalk out. Three J'kyricks. Big ones. They're dressed in tight black clothing with the sheen of silk. The one in the middle has their hands behind their back in an almost regal manner. They sniff the surrounding air while the other two scan the area with rifles I've never seen before.

Like the ship, the weapons appear to be cobbled together from spare parts.

Jay rushes over, greeting them in an elaborate display of low growls and clicks. The middle J'kyrick, the one who I assume is in charge, reaches out, grabbing Jay's snout. They touch their own snout to Jay's. A greeting, perhaps. They slowly part as Jay makes a series of grunts then points to me and Annie.

"Ace, this isn't good," Annie says, her body tense.

She has a handgun attached to her thigh. During the battle with Jay, she hasn't had the chance to use it. Now, I see her fingers flexing, hovering just over the grip of the weapon. I reach out, slowly wrapping my fingers around her hand.

"We'll be okay," I whisper.

The lead J'kyrick walks our way, with Jay in tow. The other two stay near the pod, their weapons still scanning the area. Annie squeezes my hand tightly. I wince in pain but don't make a sound.

"Greetings," the lead J'kyricks says in my own language. I blink in surprise. He then takes a small bow. Another surprise.

"Uh... greetings," I reply. "You speak Greymenia?"

"I do," the J'kyrick replies. "It is good to know the language of my enemy."

"Ace," Annies says. "What's it saying?"

"That your hair is a lovely shade of red," I reply.

Annie snorts, then shakes her head. "You're such an ass. Are we..."

"We're okay," I say. "For now. Just let me talk." I turn back to the J'kyrick. "About the whole genocide of your species thing. That was way before my time. If I had been there, though,

I would have shut that shit down. I would have looked my mother square in the eyes and said, 'not cool!'"

The lead J'kyrick raises a claw, and I stop speaking. I don't even intend to shut up. The J'kyrick just has that aura about them. Definitely royalty.

"I am aware you were not involved," the J'kyrick says. "My son tells me you have assisted him."

"Son?"

"Yes. I am Lord Inell-Za. This is my son, Prince Inell-Raz."

"My apologies," I say, dropping to my knees and pulling Annie down with me. "Your majesty."

"What the hell is going on, Ace?" she asks through gritted teeth.

"They're royalty," I reply.

"Oh, shit," Annie says, practically curling up into a ball.

"Please, rise" Lord Inell-Za says, then in English to Annie. "You as well, human. We should both be bowing to Lord Zell Ita, anyway."

"What the hell is he talking about?" Annie says as we get to our feet.

"Nothing," I say, laughing nervously. I slice a hand across my throat in the intergalactic gesture for shutting it.

"My son tells me you have been imprisoned here as well," Lord Inell-Za continues.

"That is true, your majesty."

"He tells me you allowed him to contact us."

"I did, your majesty. Along with this human here. She's a friend."

Lord Inell-Za nods to Annie, who lets out a nervous chuckle.

"You are welcome to travel with us," he says to me.

"Excuse me?" I say.

"We are taking my son to join us in our search of a new homeworld. We considered Earth, briefly, but there's too much... vegetation. Plus, humans are now friends."

He nods to Annie again, who hasn't stopped chuckling.

"Uh... thank you," I say. "But I will stay here. I have to right some wrongs I have done."

"Admirable," Lord Inell-Za says. "Let us hope your family will someday see things as you do."

"One can dream, your majesty."

"Know this, Prince Zell Ita. If you require anything. No matter what it is. We will come to your aid."

I flinch in surprise. "Seriously? Like, if I need a ride home from the airport at midnight and I call you, you'll come pick me up?"

"I do not know what this airport is, but yes."

"And if I want Chick-Fil-A on a Sunday, you'll make that happen?"

"Don't push your luck, Ace," Annie says with a false smile.

"Sorry," I say. "Lord Inell-Za, your offer is most gracious. Thank you."

"Thank you for returning my son to me."

With that, Lord Inell-Za turns to leave. Jay begins to follow, then pauses and turns back to Annie and me. He raises a claw and gives us a small wave.

"Thank you," he says.

"You're welcome," I say.

"Human," Jay says. "Apologies for your fallen comrades."

Annie jaw clenches. “I'd be lying if I said I don't hate you for that. But I hate the people who tortured you and forced you to kill more."

Jay bares his teeth. Annie and I flinch. It takes me a second to realize it's another classic J'kyrick smile.

Jay turns to follow his father. The other two J'kyrick follow suit and they all disappear into the doorway. The door closes, then the pod lifts off.

As soon as it docks with the mothership, the large craft slowly rises above the clouds. We watch as the lights eventually disappear.

The mothership is gone.

Annie lets out a huge sigh of relief. “That was insane!” she says.

“I know!”

I feel light-headed. I drop to the ground, my head between my legs.

“You know we need to have a BIG talk, *your majesty*?” Annie says with a smile.

“I know, I know.”

“Good," she says, tapping my arm. "Put your human face on. The calvary is here.”

I follow Annie's gaze, seeing lights approaching in the distance. The A.I.B. has arrived.

As always, right on time.

Chapter 37

I change my appearance back to that of Ace Trakker: International Alien of Mystery. Annie hands me my wig, brushing off dirt and leaves. When I'm confident I look presentable, I give Cabbie the go-ahead to awaken the other two agents.

They rouse with a compliment of groans.

"What happened?" one of them asks.

I turn away, whistling, content to let Annie handle this.

"We'll have a full debrief later," Annie explains. "But long story short, the J'kyrick knocked you two out, then left. It's off-world."

That leads to a flurry of more questions, which Annie does her best to answer without revealing too much.

I keep my eyes focused on the lights in the night sky. The sound of the rotors increases along with my anxiety. I'm not sure what kind of helicopters they are. Blackhawks maybe. I keep telling myself they're not here for me. If that were the case, then Annie would have arrested me already.

I turn back to her with the two agents. She's sent them on a perimeter check, no doubt tired of their questions. When she notices me looking her way, she raises an eyebrow.

"What?" she asks.

I shake my head. "Nothing. Just... thanks for believing in me."

Her expression softens as she places a hand on my shoulder. She gives it a light squeeze. Well, light to her. To me, it hurts.

"You didn't make it easy," Annie says. "But I'm glad it worked out alright in the end."

The chopper arrives in a wash of noise and light. Annie waves into the brightness, signaling we're okay. The helicopter circles the area for a moment, then disappears behind the trees. A few minutes later, a dozen A.I.B. agents, all decked out in armor similar to Annie's, burst through the treeline.

Instinctively, I raise my hands.

Annie grabs my wrist, lowering my arms.

"Sorry," I say. "Nervous habit."

"You're safe now," Annie says, as she approaches the incoming agents.

"Ma'am," one agent says with a nod. "Are you okay?"

"I'm fine," Annie replies. "There are two other agents checking the perimeter. Give them an assist."

"We're on it," the agent replies, motioning for a handful of others to follow.

The remaining agents search the area, collecting evidence, taking pictures, and scanning for any other life forms. I just stand, holding my breath.

Annie must sense my discomfort. "If those things could detect you," she whispers. "We would have known about you a long time ago."

I release a breath, my mind only mildly at ease.

"Thanks," I say.

Once the immediate area is secure, a few agents pull Annie away for questioning. I'm about to call Cabbie when another agent approaches me. He's decked out in the same futuristic armor as the others, but something seems off. It takes me a moment to realize he's the only one not armed.

"Mr. Trakker?" the agent asks, his voice cultured and refined. Definitely different from the other agents. This guy sounds like he should be sipping martinis on a beach with supermodels.

"Yea, that's me," I reply.

"Please stay where you are," Cultured and Refined says. "The Director would like to speak with you."

"Marisol's here?" I ask, flabbergasted.

"*The Director* is here," he corrects me.

"Sure. Sorry. I'll stay put."

He gives me a sharp nod then turns to join the other agents. A few seconds later, Marisol exits the treeline, dressed in her trademark black suit. As always, she exudes an air of leadership and confidence. I notice a few of the agents straighten a little as she passes them.

"Ace," she says, stopping a few feet away.

"Marisol," I reply with a nod.

"I told you to merely report the location."

Marisol is all business now. Her tone professional and clipped. I don't know whether to be scared or just go with it.

I decide to do both.

"I did," I say. "But things got a little hairy. I had to act fast."

"I see. Agent Quinn relays you were able to talk the J'kyrick out of destroying our planet."

"How do you know that? You just got here." I point to the edge of the treeline. "Annie is still over there talking to your agents as we speak."

"I hear what they hear," Marisol says, tapping her right ear.

"Ah. Must be disorienting having a conversation while listening to another conversation."

Marisol shrugs. "You get used to it. Now, tell me. How did you prevent the annihilation of Earth?"

Then it hits me. I prevented the annihilation of Earth. I saved the world. At least I think I did. Was the world really in danger to begin with? If I never showed up, Jay would have likely just gone home.

But what if he didn't? What if he told his father of the atrocities humankind had subjected him to? What if I had never told him my story? Jay was a rage filled murder machine. It's likely he could have just told his dad to nuke the planet from orbit.

Maybe, just maybe, my little act of kindness prevented that.

"Um. I guess I did," I say. "He just wanted to go home. I think he needed to talk to someone who wasn't trying to kill him or force him to kill."

Marisol stiffens. Like most things she does, it's subtle. I catch it though. Either because of my heightened senses or my familiarity with Marisol, I don't know. But I catch it. If she knows about whatever black ops project Jay was part of, she doesn't say.

Marisol quickly recovers and offers a small smile. "I suppose this country... this planet... owes you a great deal of gratitude."

I'm a little shocked. Not so much by Marisol's statement. But by how it makes me feel. I feel... good. Like stupid grin on my face good. I started this bounty hunting journey to right my wrongs. It may take a while to right them all, but this is a start.

"Does that mean I can have whatever I want?" I ask. "Like a lifetime supply of Reese's Pieces?"

Marisol's smile grows wider. “I think that can be arranged. However, I thought you would want something a little more substantial.”

I shrug. “I’m a simple alie... man. I’m a man. A simple human man.”

Marisol laughs. “Thank you, Ace. Seriously. I don’t know what you did or how you did it. But your saved a lot of lives.. Thank you.”

“You’re welcome," I say, fight back tears. I don't want Marisol to know she's making me emotional. I'll never live it down. "Oh, and Annie knows. About this.” I point to my face.

“Oh,” Marisol says.

“Yea.”

“I’ll smooth it over with her.”

“She seems pretty chill about it.”

“Have you ever known Agent Quinn to be chill about anything?”

“Good point.," I say. "Thanks. So... I’m free to go?”

“You are," Marisol nods. "I’ll call you tomorrow. You’ll have to come in for a full debrief. But it’s late and I’m sure you’re tired.”

“Alright then,” I say. “See ya later, water dwelling reptile!”

“That’s not how that goes," Marisol sighs. "You know what, nevermind. Bye, Ace.”

As I turn to leave, I send a mental call to Cabbie. He's already waiting at the bottom of the hill. I can already tell it's a different Cabbie based on the car. When I climb into the backseat, I further confirm this is a different Cabbie because he hasn't been graced with any of my little presents.

“Hey Ace,” Cabbie says.

"Hey Cabbie," I say, reaching into my pocket. "Here, I got something for you."

Cabbie takes the orb with a smile, then leans over and puts it in the glove box.

"Where to?" he asks.

"Anywhere but here."

I lean back, looking out the window. The night sky. The stars. Sometimes I miss it. Traveling between worlds. But for the first time in a long time, I feel like this is just where I need to be.

Chapter 38

"Authorities are calling the event an unauthorized rave thrown by a local DJ. You can see from the footage here that multiple partygoers flooded Mount Jacinto State Park for the impromptu and illegal party. According to sources close to the scene, holographic technology was used to simulate a giant spaceship hovering over the state park. Authorities want to stress once again, do not be alarmed. Any lights or ships that were seen were just part of the show. We'll keep you updated as more unfolds. Now onto our next news story. Is your cat telepathic? New research suggests..."

I close the news app and pocket my phone. I can't help but smile. Not because I'm pretty sure I saw Annie in the news footage as one of the ravers. Which I remind myself to give her crap about later. I'm not even smiling at the swiftness with which the A.I.B. has covered up the J'kyrick mother ship.

I'm smiling because I saved the freaking world! At least I think I did. I'll go with yes I did.

It feels good for several reasons. One of which is, myself and everyone else on this planet are alive. That's always a good thing. The second reason is I've broken away from Mother's rule. At least partially. I've never been fully on board with invading planets, yet that's what I was sent here to do. When that didn't happen, the human race lived their lives in peace, never knowing of the looming Greymenian threat. Now that I've saved this planet, I feel like it's mine. Not because I've conquered it. But because I've cared for it.

It's a new feeling, but a welcome one.

Smiling intensifies.

My phone chirps.

I take it out of my pocket, reading the notification.

LINDERMAN: Do you have the orb?

In all of the excitement, I forgot I was supposed to retrieve the orb for Linderman. I gave it to Cabbie, well one of the Cabbie's, as a gift. I'll just mind call him later and have him drop it off at Linderman's office.

Right now, I'm just going to enjoy the ride.

Cabbie has offered to take me anywhere I want to go. It doesn't take me long to come up with an answer. Honestly, there's only one place I want to be right now.

I walk into Alissa‘s house. The early morning sunlight casts piercing shards of light across the living room. Lonnie's not on the couch, likely moved to one of the spare bedrooms. It would be a shame if someone rang the doorbell, then peeked inside as Alissa opened the door to reveal a giant alien crab spider thing on the couch.

I chuckle at the thought.

If only humans knew the insanity that's happening on their planet. Even before us aliens came along, there was a bunch of weirdness. The Loch Ness Monster. Not one of us. The Bermuda Triangle. Definitely odd, but not alien in origin. Humans don't even understand the entirety of their own oceans. There's no way they can understand the complexity of interstellar beings.

Hopefully, they'll never have to.

“Hello!” I call out.

Footsteps echo from the kitchen.

Alissa turns the corner, a surprised look on her face.

"You're okay," she says. It's more of a statement than a question.

"Yup," I say. "Why? Did you think I was dead?"

"Yes!" she exclaims, then rushes to me, pulling me into a hug.

I wrap my arms around her, happy that someone else is happy to see me. I don't get that very often. We part as Alissa wipes her eyes.

"When we didn't hear from you," she says. "I thought the worst. Then I saw the news, and I just knew Mom had something to do with the coverup."

I laugh. "Yea that was a bit extreme. But I'm fine. How are you?"

"I'm great now that I know you're okay. I wish you would have told me the world was ending, though."

"Sorry, but your mother..."

Alissa rolls her eyes. "Yea, I figured. Lonnie filled me in when I woke up." She's been in this position before. It's hard being the daughter of the director of a supersecret government agency.

"How's he doing, anyway?" I ask.

Alissa gives me a look, then leads me to the garage. She flips a light switch, then waves a hand to the empty space. I try not to laugh.

There's a huge hole in the concrete floor.

"That jerk," I say.

"I know, right," Alissa replies with a sigh.

I shake my head. "He shouldn't be digging in his condition."

"Ace, what about the huge hole in my foundation!?"

"Oh yea. That too. Just don't get it fixed. He only tunnels into places he likes. So he'll be back."

Alissa blows air sharply out of nose. "Great. That won't be scary at all. A giant alien crab standing at the foot of my bed in the middle of the night asking for some water."

"He likes Dr. Pepper."

"Good to know," Alissa says, shaking her head. "Good to know."

I laugh as we walk back into the house. I've been on this planet a long time and have lived even longer. I'm not an expert on the human race. I skipped most of my Earth Studies classes in high school. But I've learned a lot during my time here. A lot about what humans like to do, what they like to eat and watch. It's all fascinating stuff but none of it is as fascinating as the connections they make.

For Alissa to take me in as a member of her family says a lot about humans. Sure, there are some terrible ones out there. But that could be said of any species.

Surround yourself with the ones you love, and the ones who love you, and you'll never be alone.

No matter what planet you're on.

Epilogue

Matthew Linderman stares at the screen in equal parts reverence and disbelief. It‘s really him. The progeny of his employer. The one who will rule when The Queen is gone. Regardless of Linderman's power, by his birthright, the being on the screen in front of him is to be respected.

“How can I help you, my Lord?” Linderman says to the screen.

The face, partly covered in shadow, leans forward, revealing the grey skin. The black eyes.

“We received a signal from Earth,” the Prince says. “It was strong. So strong it reached all the way to a J’kyrick fleet just outside of your solar system.”

“Yes, my Lord," Linderman lowers his head. "That is my mistake. It was the orb of creation. I removed it from the Earth to make some modifications. It was stolen from my lab.”

“Why would you do this?” the Prince asks. "Why remove it from the Earth? Won't that cause... instability?"

To Linderman's surprise, the tone isn’t accusatory. It’s quite the opposite, actually. The Prince seems to be genuinely curious.

Linderman fights to urge to explain how the orbs work. How when the population of Earth grows, the orbs must be updated to accommodate the excess bodies. The orbs must also say because your family left me here to die. Because I‘m lonely. Because, although I have humans and other aliens to speak with, none of them can know who I really am.

"I was tested a new deep range communication, Sire," Linderman lies. "So that I may be able to communicate with you anywhere on the planet. Instead of only down here in my basement."

The Grey Man nods, seemingly satisfied by this answer. He rubs his chin, consulting something off-screen.

"The J'kyrick," the Grey Man finally says. "They should be extinct, yes?"

"Yes, my Lord."

"Why aren't they?"

"I do not know, my Lord. Judging from the ship, it appears a few escaped. They must have been living on the ship for generations, growing their numbers."

"Do you think they will attack?" The Grey man asks.

"Attack?"

"Yes. Do you think my homeworld is in danger?"

"I... I don't believe so. They wouldn't be foolish enough to try. You already destroyed them once. I have no doubt it can be done again."

The Grey Man nods again. Linderman wonders why the Prince asked the question. Surely he knows no being in the universe would be stupid enough to oppose his family's empire.

"They are a slippery bunch," the Prince says. "Not unlike Earth's cockroaches, hm?"

"Yes, sire. Insects indeed." Linderman weighs his next comment carefully. "May I ask a question?"

The grey Man raises a hairless brow. "Speak."

"Why were the J'kyrick hunted to extinction in the first place?"

The Grey Man taps the armrest, his eyes focusing on something off screen. He sits that way for a long moment. So long Linderman suspects the transmission froze.

Finally, the Grey Man smiles. "They... didn't fall in line. We asked for their complete allegiance to us and they declined."

"Ah. I see. Thank you, my Lord."

"Does that satisfy your curiosity?" the Grey Man asks with an edge in his voice. Linderman knows he is not to ask anything like that again.

Linderman nods. "It does my Lord. Apologies if I was out of line."

The Prince waves a hand dismissively. "It is quite alright, Architect. Or whatever name it is you go by now."

"It's Linderman. Matthew Linderman."

"Ah yes. Linderman. Tell me, how is the solar system these days when not sullied by the likes of J'kyricks."

"All is well, my Lord. The project on Earth's moon is nearing completion."

"Ah, the deep space communication array. Do you believe it will work?"

"I do, my Lord. One step closer in preparing Earth for first contact."

"And then the interstellar lanes will be open to commerce?"

"Yes, my Lord."

Linderman knows there is more to it than commerce. On the outside, the Greymenians present themselves as a wealthy royal family. Their riches gained by opening up worlds to interstellar commerce. Linderman knows better. Sure, money is a huge part of it. But so is the suffering. What the Greymenians don't let others know is they conquer worlds, enslaving the population, forcing them into labor.

If Ace had not been captured when he first crashed here, this world would already be lost.

"What other news?" The Grey Man asks, his tone bored.

"Your sister is here."

He perks up at this revelation. "Oh? Which one? I have dozens."

"Yes, of course," Linderman says. "I believe it to be Zell Otula."

The Prince snorts a laugh. "She always was a rebellious one. What is she doing on Earth?"

"She is not Earth, my Lord. She resides on the next planet over. Mars."

"I see," the Prince says. "That is interesting. Does my brother know?"

"He is unaware."

"Good. Keep it that way. What stupid moniker has he adopted again?"

"Trakker, my Lord. Ace Trakker."

"Idiot."

"Yes, my Lord."

"You know, I believe it's time I paid him a visit." The Prince smiles. "It's been so long."

A shiver runs down Linderman's spine. "Yes, my Lord."

"Prepare for my arrival. Keep it quiet."

"As you wish, my..."

The screen goes dark. Linderman shakes his head. Of course, the Prince hung up. He always has to have the last word. Another shiver runs through Linderman's body.

Lord Zell Itull is coming here. To Earth. Normally, that wouldn't bother Linderman. Greymenians have always visited the planets in which they rule. Yet something about this visit feels off.

Perhaps because this is the first time that Linderman can recall that there will be three Greymenians in the same solar system.

Where the Prince and his family go, trouble will undoubtedly follow.

Also By

Coming Soon

False Gods – Book 3 of The False Idols Saga

Books

False Idols – Book 1 of the False Idols Saga

False Prophets – Book 2 of the False Idols Saga

Somnium: The Dream

Short Stories by a Short Author

Short Stories

Monolith

The Storming of Area 51

Acknowledgments

First, I want to thank my wife for going along with whatever crazy thing I think of.

Thank you to the graphic designers and editors who helped to make my dream a reality.

Finally, thank you to all of my friends and family who encouraged me to pursue a career in writing. Regardless of how this journey ends, your kind words and support mean more than you'll know.

About Author

Thank you so much for reading *Ace Tracker: Alien Bounty Hunter.*

If you enjoyed this book, please leave a review. As an indie author, reviews are essential for me to continue writing. They help other readers find my work and let me know what I can do to improve.

If you want to check out any of my other works, head to my website: https://markdamonbrooks.com[1]

Connect with me on social media!

Facebook: https://www.facebook.com/mdamonbrooks

X (Twitter): https://twitter.com/mdamonbrooks

Instagram: http://www.instagram.com/mdamonbrooks[2]

Bookbub: https://www.bookbub.com/profile/mark-damon-brooks

---

1. https://www.markdamonbrooks.com
2. https://www.instagram.com/mdamonbrooks/

Milton Keynes UK
Ingram Content Group UK Ltd.
UKHW020650201123
432908UK00019B/2374

9 798223 251439